Natural Magic

The Moon Tree. The origin of this magical design is found in the art of ancient Assyria. This version symbolises the Moon in her monthly passage through the twelve Signs of the Zodiac. The words "Magna Mater" mean "Great Mother".

Natural Magic

DOREEN VALIENTE

PHOENIX PUBLISHING INC.

By the same author:

An ABC of Witchcraft
Witchcraft for Tomorrow
The Rebirth of Witchcraft

PHOENIX PUBLISHING, INC.
P.O. Box 3829
Blaine, Washington USA 98231
www.phoenixpublishing.com

Published in the U.K. by
ROBERT HALE LTD.
45-47 Clerkenwell Green
London EC1R 0HT

ISBN 0-919345-80-8

Cover design by Richard Bakker

Printed in the U.S.A.

Contents

Illustrations

CREDITS

Author's own drawings: 1, 2, 4, 8; from *Observations on Popular Antiquities* by John Brand (Chatto and Windus, London, 1877): 3, 9, 12, 13, 15; from *Our Woodland Trees* by Francis George Heath (Sampson Low & Co., London, 1878): 5 (artist L. Evans); from *Le Satanisme et la Magie* by Jules Bois (Leon Chailley, Paris, 1895): 6, 7, 10 (artist Henri de Malvost); from *Etruscan Roman Remains* by Charles Godfrey Leland (Fisher Unwin, London, 1892): 11, 14, 16; from *The Book of Days* (W. & R. Chambers, Edinburgh, 1869): 17; from *The Discovery of Witches* by Matthew Hopkins (London, 1647): 18.

Foreword

To many people, the title of this book may seem to be a contradiction in terms. They think of magic as something essentially unnatural; indeed, against nature, because if it works at all then it must work by overthrowing nature's laws.

However, the occult philosophers of olden time have never conceived of magic in this way. To them, magic works because of nature's laws, not in spite of them. It is something built into the universe. Hence, there is nothing really supernatural or supernormal, in the strict sense of these words. All is part of nature; but much of the realm of nature is 'occult', that is, hidden.

The occultist, therefore, is one who ventures into these hidden realms in search of their secrets. He is not some wild-eyed crank who goes around dressed in eccentric clothes in order to attract attention to himself. Some people may behave like this, and no doubt get a lot of fun out of it. They are perhaps feeling the influence of Uranus, the planet of the eccentric and bizarre (among other things), which rules the new age of Aquarius upon which mankind is entering. However, in the past occultists have been more anxious to go about their business secretly than to call attention to themselves. When the penal laws against witchcraft were in force, becoming noticed as a practitioner of the occult could have dire results.

Today, it must be evident to all thinking people that we have entered upon a new era. Call it the Age of Aquarius, the Aeon of Horus (as Aleister Crowley did), or what you will. Not only has the physical world been revolutionized by new scientific discoveries; things like morality and basic social attitudes are undergoing change. One of the spheres in which this is happening is the public attitude to occultism.

It would not be an exaggeration to say that a revival of magic has taken place. It started around 1951, when the last of the moth-eaten old Witchcraft Acts was finally banished from the statute book of English law. Hitherto, this Act had been used to prosecute Spiritualist mediums and clairvoyants, and in theory it could be used to bring a prosecution irrespective of whether a medium was genuine or not. Its repeal and replacement by the Fraudulent Mediums Act, which in effect legally recognizes the possibility of genuine psychic gifts, was a turning-point in the history of occultism in Britain. Not only did it set Spiritualism free; it also, perhaps rather to the surprise of the legislators, enabled witchcraft itself to emerge from the shadows where it had lurked for so long, and to be proclaimed by its followers as the oldest religion in the world.

In the same fateful year, 1951, appeared the first edition (published by Riders of London) of *The Great Beast*, John Symonds' now-famous biography of Aleister Crowley, a man of considerable stature as a poet who had devoted his whole amazing life to magic. This book caught the public imagination and from then on the occult revival has steadily gathered momentum.

The results of this have naturally been mixed. People who had become cynically atheist and materialist because of their disgust with orthodox religions, have been encouraged to think again and have sometimes been enabled to achieve a completely new outlook upon life. On the other hand, all kinds of charlatanry have been enabled to flourish; and, of course, the hustlers have moved in, determined to get their hands upon every possible pound or dollar available in this great new bonanza.

It is partly as a protest against this latter tendency that this book has been written. I wanted to show people that magic is for all, as nature is for all. Magic, indeed, is all around us, in stones, flowers, stars, the dawn wind and the sunset cloud; all we need is the ability to see and understand. We do not need to join high-sounding 'secret' fraternities, swear frightful oaths and pay fees, in order to become magicians. Very few fraternities are genuinely old and still fewer have any real secrets to impart. Still less do we need to buy a load of expensive paraphernalia, such as ceremonial swords, wands and so on, which can be seen advertised tor sale today.

Moreover, I have tried in this book to be essentially practical, as magicians and witches have been throughout the ages, ever since the days of ancient Egypt and before. Magic is meant to help people, including yourself. The priggish notion that 'you mustn't use magic for yourself, only to help others' is a piece of sanctimonious waffle that is entirely modern. If you study the history of magic and the lives of famous magicians, you will find that this is so. The highly spiritual religion of ancient Egypt was inextricably entwined with magic, as the great Egyptologist Wallis Budge has made clear in his book *Egyptian Magic* (first published in London in 1901 and now reprinted by Dover Publications, Inc., New York, 1971).

Many people will tell you that occultism, witchcraft and magic are dangerous. So they are; so is crossing the road; but we shall not get far if we are afraid ever to attempt it. However, we can choose either to dash across recklessly, or to use our common sense and cross with care, and so it is with magic. It is often argued, too, that magic can be used both for good and for evil. Of course it can; so can electricity, atomic power, television, the power of the press, indeed anything that has any power in it at all.

However, in my book I have endeavoured to exclude anything really harmful and where any caution is necessary, I have tried to indicate it. I have set out to write a treatise which will put the simpler kinds of magic, such as the village 'wise-women', or white witches, have used for centuries, within the reach of all.

For this reason, too, I have written about the old method of fortune-telling with ordinary playing cards, rather than the more expensive Tarot cards; because almost everyone has a pack of playing cards in their home, or can easily obtain one. It may be wondered what relation playing cards have to natural magic; but I think the curious correspondence noted in Chapter X between the pack of cards and the calendar of the year earns them a place here.

The quotation in Chapter V of part of the wonderful 'Hymn to the Sun' by the Pharaoh Akhenaton, is from the translation of this hymn made by the late Professor Henry James Breasted, and comes from his book *A History of Egypt*, first published in 1906 (Hodder & Stoughton, London, and Charles Scribner's Sons, USA).

As poetry is essentially a magical art, and has its origins in magic, here is a poem of my own which seems relevant in this place. It is entitled "The Mysteries":

Here and now are the Mysteries.
Out of no stored and storied past
Of things long lost;
But the breathing moment of time.
Out of no twilight
But that which falls upon the hills this night.
The old trees partake of them,
And the voices of the grass;
The ghost-white blossomed elders,
And the first clouded glow
Of the rising moon.
If we can hear,
If we can see,
Out of no buried past they come;
But from the fields of our own home
Is reaped the grain
That makes the bread of their feast.
Out of the flowers of every summer
Flows the honey of their mead.
Look, between the stones is a blade of grass;
And all the rites of the high Mysteries,
And the runes of all witcheries,
Are written upon it.

DOREEN VALIENTE

I

Magic of the Mind

What does one need to work magic?

Many of the old books called grimoires, secretly handed down through the centuries, tell their readers of most elaborate requirements for the rites of magic. They describe consecrated swords, wands, pentacles and so on, together with rare incenses and other strange formulae. But the greatest adepts in the magical art have also made it clear that all these things are but the outward trappings. The real magic is in the human mind.

Cornelius Agrippa, one of the most famous magicians of olden times, says in his writings: "Unless a man be born a magician, and God have destined him even from his birth to the work, so that spirits do willingly come of their own accord — which doth happen to few — a man must use only of those things herein set down, or written in our other books of occult philosophy, as means to fix the mind upon the work to be done; for it is in the power of the mind itself that spirits do come and go, and magical works are done, and all things in nature are but as uses to induce the will to rest upon the point desired."

The mind, then, is the greatest instrument of magic. Nor do we need to go back to the middle ages in order to see it at work. One of the most remarkable *public* demonstrations of what the ancients would certainly have called magic was given on 12th September 1954, at Orillia, Ontario, Canada.

The magician on this occasion was Dr Rolf Alexander, a New Zealander who graduated in medicine at Prague, and later became a pupil of the famous and mysterious philosopher, Gurdjieff. The witnesses of his demonstration were the Mayor of Orillia and more than fifty other leading citizens. Moreover, proof that what they saw was no illusion is provided by a series of independent press photographs.

The demonstration took place outdoors, and consisted of disintegrating and dispersing clouds by the power of the mind. One of the observers was asked to select a group of cumulus clouds. This was then photographed. Another observer was asked to indicate a particular cloud from this group as the target. Dr Alexander concentrated upon this target cloud while the photographers continued to take pictures at intervals. The experiment commenced at 2.09 pm. By 2.17 pm the target cloud had disintegrated and practically vanished, while other neighbouring cloud-groups remained in the sky. As Dr Alexander pointed out in his book, there can be no collusion between a man and a cloud. (*The Power of the Mind*, by Rolf Alexander, MD, Werner Laurie, London 1956).

In 1956 Dr Alexander came to Britain and repeated his successful experiments in disintegrating clouds at Holne Tor, in Devonshire and on Hampstead Heath. His efforts were photographed and televised, and an article about him entitled "Cloud Buster", by Fyfe Robertson, appeared in *Picture Post*, in the issue dated 30th June 1956.

The magic and mystery of the human mind, and its hidden powers, have intrigued philosophers throughout history, from ancient Egypt to the most modern laboratories for the study of parapsychgology — a number of which, incidentally, exist in officially materialist Russia. Parapsychology means that which goes beyond the science of psychology, as generally accepted. It is a modern synonym for psychical research. Both terms are simply long words for things we can't explain.

Hitler was very interested in the study of occult powers. During the Second World War, he set up a special department to investigate them. This was known as the Tattva Department, from an oriental word *tattva*, meaning one of the subtle powers of the universe which are characterized as fire, water, air, earth and aether.

On the side of the Allies, covens of British witches gathered together at Lammas, 1940, screened by the trees of the New Forest, in order to work their rites against Hitler's threatened invasion.

We generally believe the findings of modern psychology

with regard to the dual mind of man, conscious and subconscious, to be a great modern discovery. Yet the ancient Egyptians explained the human entity as being composed of a number of principles, which is certainly a comparable idea. The Egyptians taught that man was sevenfold. They told of the *khat*, or material body, which when mummified and entombed with the proper rites became a *sahu*, or glorified body, by means of which a link could be preserved with the departed. But man also had a non-material body, the *ka*, or astral double, and another mysterious vehicle, the *khaibit* or shadow. His vitality and emotions dwelt in the *ab*, or heart; and incidentally our way of regarding the heart as the seat of the emotions derives from this belief of ancient Egypt. The vitality itself was called *sekhem*. The rational soul or mind of man was symbolized as the *ba*, represented as a human-headed bird. His divine and imperishable spirit was called the *khu*, a shining essence of light.

Psychologists of the school of Jung consider that to the principles of conscious and subconscious mind should be added a third, the superconscious, or Greater Self. This is evidently analogous to the *khu* of ancient Egyptian belief.

Today, psychologists are looking at ancient myths and legends with new eyes. They perceive in the stories of descents into the shadowy underworld, hell, or Hades, an analogy with the depths of the subconscious mind. Rising upwards into the shining heights of heaven is analogous with contacting the realms of higher consciousness. Man bears heaven and hell within himself. This again is an old tenet of occult philosophy, namely that man is the microcosm, or little universe, and all that is without him is also within.

Before we can work magic, we must understand what magic is and what we are. We have seen that magic is the power of the mind, for good or ill, and we must look into the mind to find the true magical instruments. The great injunction of the Greek Mysteries, which were derived from the Egyptian, was *Gnothi se auton*, "Know thyself".

The pre-eminence of Egypt in magical matters is shown by a saying of the ancient world: "Ten measures of magic were given to the world. Egypt took nine. The rest took one."

If, therefore, we wish for instruction in magic of our western

European world, we will do well to look towards Egypt. There was a connection between ancient Egypt and ancient Britain, as Egyptian beads found in the barrows of the Salisbury Plain area prove. We know today that Britain's prehistoric stone monuments, particularly Stonehenge, are much more sophisticated structures than was previously thought. The possibility is that both ancient Egypt and ancient Europe, especially the British Isles, derive their oldest culture from a common source now sunk beneath the waves, the wondrous Atlantis.

Great though their traditions are, the ways of the East are more suited to the peoples of the East than they are to western bodies and minds. It would be a pity for us to long for the treasures of India and Tibet, and ignore the riches to be found as the rightful heritage of our own races of the west.

Many people take up the study of occultism because they want to develop psychic or magical powers, in order to change their lives. There is nothing wrong with this, provided they understand one thing: *the only way you can really change your life is by changing yourself.*

One often encounters people who have an attitude to magic which assumes, more or less, that if only they could find the way to make some mighty talisman that would grant all their wishes — or at least, enable them to win the top dividend of the football pool — everything would be different. But it wouldn't; they themselves would still be the same and with the same personal problems still hung about their necks. For instance, a silly woman who was always making herself miserable over some man would be just the same, poor or rich. A man who was perpetually greedy and discontented would still be discontented, however much money he had, because he didn't know how to be happy.

There is an old saying: "The adept owns nothing, yet he has the use of everything." The meaning of this is that the adept knows that everything in the world may be at his service, to use and enjoy for the good of himself and others — yet it is only *loaned* to him for a time, by the powers of nature and destiny. It came originally from nature and to nature it will return. Pondering upon this truth, the adept ceases to be selfish and greedy. Knowing himself to be forever linked and united with the Cosmic Mind, he ceases to be insecure — subconscious feelings of insecurity being the roots of selfishness and greed. With a liberated mind, he is able to draw to himself the things he needs, by developing will-power, imagination, concentration and faith.

In the late eighteenth century there lived a remarkable man called Mehmet Karagoz. He was known as the Wizard of Albania. People from all over Europe and Asia sought his advice and told stories of his supernormal powers. He was born in the wild and remote mountains of Tartary, and his father was a shaman, a magician-priest of the primitive religion of those parts.

When he was a young man, Mehmet seemed to be so lacking in natural ability that his father felt unable to have him initiated, thinking that the youth was incapable at that time of following his father's vocation. Instead, the old shaman gave Mehmet a piece of practical instruction: "Believe in the possibility of what you intend to do, hold it strongly in your mind, and it will happen." He told his son to practise constantly and one day he would find that the power had indeed developed and was his.

This instruction of his father's was the foundation of Mehmet Karagoz's magical career. He travelled widely in search of knowledge and eventually settled in Albania, where he founded his own occult school and became one of the most famous and most mysterious of adepts. He used no rituals, but worked entirely through the powers of the mind.

But how are the powers of the mind to be awakened? We are told much of the great importance of will-power, concentration and so on; how can these qualities be developed?

Much depends on how much in earnest people really are and on how much time they are prepared to give to the pursuit. There is a great difference between willing something and just weakly wishing it. For instance — will you spend an evening in meditation and study, or can you just not resist watching that show on television? Do you want to buy that book that may teach you something valuable — or must you spend your money instead on the latest fashion, or a few rounds of drinks with the boys? Only the persons themselves can answer these questions.

However, if you really want to commune with your own inner mind, there are certain times which are particularly useful. One of these is at night, when you are on the borderline between waking and sleep, and this is a time when ideas can be suggested by you to your subconscious mind, with a great degree of success.

The discoverer of this method was Charles Godfrey Leland, the great American collector of folklore, and one of the most original minds of his day. His book entitled *Have You a Strong Will?* first appeared in 1899. It was subtitled: *How to develop and strengthen will power, memory, or any other faculty or attribute of the mind, by the easy process of self-hypnotism.*

Leland was an old man when he made this discovery, and its great benefit to himself, as recorded in his letters, made him put it into a book. His process involves no dramatic struggles for will-power, but rather a gentle and cheerful resolution to develop the qualities you desire. Then at night, when you are lying comfortably in bed, and just on the borderland of sleep, saying to yourself over and over again, as if repeating a lesson, that tomorrow you *will* be more strong-willed, cheerful, better-tempered, or whatever quality it is that you desire.

Pass into sleep with this idea in your mind, and it will grow in the depths of your subconscious like a seed planted in the earth. Persistence in this practice will encourage its growth and its ultimate flowering in your life. Leland found, too, that he could awaken new faculties of awareness in himself by this method, which as a writer and artist he found extremely valuable.

In a letter to a relative, written in 1897, he said:

> I begin to realise in very fact that there are tremendous powers, quite unknown to us, in the mind, and that we can perhaps by long continued steady *will* awake abilities of which we never dreamed. Thus you can by repetition will yourself to notice hundreds of things which used to escape you and this soon begins to appear to be miraculous. You must will and think the things over and over as if learning a lesson, saying or rather *thinking* to yourself intently, "I will that all day tomorrow I shall notice every little thing." And though *you forget* all about it, it will not forget itself and it will haunt you, and you *will* notice all kinds of things. After doing this a dozen times, you will have a new faculty awakened.

That famous occult fraternity, the Order of the Golden Dawn, was naturally interested in the powers of the mind. In addition to the knowledge lectures and rituals, a number of papers on various subjects were circulated among members, which were called "Flying Rolls". The following are extracts from one of these papers, entitled "A Few Thoughts on Imagination". It is dated 1892, and was written by "Resurgam":

> The uninitiated interpret imagination as something "imaginary" in the popular sense of the word: that is, something unreal. But imagination is reality.
>
> When a man imagines, he actually creates a form on the astral or even on some higher plane; and this form is as real and objective to intelligent beings on that plane as our earthly surroundings are real and objective to us.
>
> This form which imagination creates may have only a transient existence, productive of no important result; or it may be vitalized and thus used for good or evil.
>
> To practise Magic both imagination and will must be called into action. They are co-equal in the work. Nay more, the imagination must precede the will, in order to produce the greatest possible effect.
>
> The will, unaided, can send forth a current, and that current cannot be wholly inoperative; yet its effect is vague and indefinite because the will unaided sends forth nothing but the current of force.
>
> The imagination unaided can create an image, and this image must have an existence of varying duration, yet can do nothing of importance unless vitalized and directed by the will.
>
> When, however, the two are conjoined, when the imagination creates an image and the will directs and uses that image, marvellous magical results may be obtained . . .
>
> N.B. Whilst it is always lawful and advisable to consult with a higher adept before any important magical work, yet in every other direction absolute secrecy must be maintained, as it tends to decentralize and dissipate the force if it is talked of to others.

Some "Notes on the above paper" were added by "Non Omnis Moriar", in which he said:

> Imagination must be distinguished from fancy; from mere roving thoughts, or empty visions. By it we now mean an orderly and intentional mental process and result. Imagination is the creative faculty of the human mind, the plastic energy, the formative power.
>
> In the language of the esoteric Theosophists, the power of imagination to create thought forms is called Kriya Sakti, that is, the mysterious power of thought which enables us to produce external, phenomenal, perceptible results by its own inherent energy when fertilized by the will.

> It is the ancient Hermetic dogma that any idea can be made to manifest externally, if only by culture the art of concentration is obtained; just similarly as an external result of action produced by a current of will force.

Some very important magical principles are contained in this paper. The significance of the ancient symbol of magic, the pentagram or five-pointed star, is that of spirit or mind ruling over the world of matter. When drawn as it should be, with one point upwards, this topmost point symbolizes spirit, the unseen, while the other four points represent the four elements, fire, water, air and earth, which the ancients regarded as making up the manifested world.

The 'Flying Rolls' of the Order of the Golden Dawn have now been collected, edited and published by Francis King, under the title of *Astral Projection, Ritual Magic and Alchemy* (Neville Spearman, London, 1971).

II
Magic of the Four Elements

The occult philosophers, magicians and alchemists of olden times regarded the material world as being composed of the four elements of fire, water, air and earth. Beyond these again was a mysterious principle called aether, the quintessence, or spirit.

Exactly the same idea is found in the occultism of the east. There the elements are called *tattvas*, and are represented as *Tejas*, the red triangle; *Apas*, the white crescent; *Vayu*, the blue circle; *Prithivi*, the yellow square; and *Akasha*, the black egg. These are the symbols of fire, water, air, earth and spirit, respectively. A composite emblem composed of these symbols may often be seen topping the spire which surmounts some ancient and time-worn sanctuary, in Tibet and elsewhere in eastern lands.

In Europe, the mysterious fraternity of the Rosicrucians were sometimes called *Philosophi per ignem*, the fire-philosophers. This is because fire to them was the symbol of transmutation. The substance of a candle becomes transmuted by burning and changes into light. By their beliefs and practices, the occult philosophers of old sought to transmute that which was base into something better, to attain illumination and enlightenment. They had a mystic saying or motto: *Igne Natura renovatur integra*, "All Nature is renewed by fire."

The candles and lamps which burn in temples and churches all over the world are not merely for the mundane purpose of giving light. Their use is part of the time honoured philosophy of fire. Magicians, too, use candles to illuminate their place of working, rather than artificial light, because of the atmosphere which the soft natural flame can give even to an everyday room.

Fire was considered to be the most spiritual of the elements, not only because of its light-giving quality, but because the use of fire is one of the things which most markedly distinguishes man from the beasts. Dancing round a ritual bonfire may well be man's most primitive ceremony. Seeing pictures in the fire was one of his earliest sources of clairvoyant vision, when the tribal groups huddled together in the darkness of the caves.

To this day, there is an old countryside belief in Somerset that leaping flames talk, and if you listen to them at the right moment, they will tell you your future. The technical name for divination by fire is *pyromancy*.

With the availability of many different coloured candles in the present day, a whole magical lore has grown up around the practice of candle-burning. Fewer people today have an open fire by which to practise pyromancy; but candle-burning for magical purposes is becoming more popular.

The practitioners of this art generally advise that you should burn your candle last thing at night, and then retire to bed with the thought in your mind that the ritual will succeed. If this time is not practicable, however, then perform the rite anywhere that you can be quiet and undisturbed.

Select a candle that is of the appropriate colour for what you are trying to do, according to the list of colours given further on in this chapter. The candle should be new, and never used for any other purpose. You should have also a little phial of anointing oil, which is likewise kept solely for magical purposes. This must be pure vegetable oil and advanced practitioners sometimes use costly scented oils. Sandalwood oil, for instance, has a beautiful scent and is suitable for magical anointing; while the strange, exciting perfume of patchouli oil is very popular in America among practitioners of voodoo.

If, however, you have none of these, then make use of pure olive oil. You may care to experiment yourself by adding aromatic herbs to the oil, plus a little gum benzoin to keep it from going rancid. However, the main purpose of anointing oil is simply to impress your thoughts upon the candle, to consecrate it, so to speak, to a particular purpose. From time immemorial, magicians have used anointing oil for

Symbolic magical design showing the Seven-pointed Star of the Seven Planets. Reading around the Star, the order of the planets' apparent motion is shown, from Saturn the slowest-moving to the Moon, the fastest. Reading along the lines of the star, the order in which the planets rule the days of the week is shown, from Sunday ruled by the Sun to Saturday ruled by Saturn. Outside the star are symbols of the four elements, Earth, Air, Fire and Water. Beneath is the Ankh Cross, the Ancient Egyptian sign of Life. Around is a wreath of flowers and foliage, representing fertility.

consecration ceremonies.

Before you start your ritual, get clear in your mind what your wish is and then write it down upon a slip of new paper. You will put this slip of paper beneath the candlestick in which your candle burns. As with all magical things, the candlestick you use for ritual purposes should be kept apart for those purposes only and not put to common use. If you buy an antique candlestick for magical ceremonies, then clean it thoroughly before you use it, to get rid of other influences that may be lingering on it.

Any other light in the room where you are working should be lowered and well shaded. Then take a little of the anointing oil upon your fingers and gently rub it upon the candle, concentrating upon the idea of imbuing the candle with your thoughts and wishes. However, do not merely rub up and down; start from the centre, and rub from the centre upwards and then from the centre downwards. Then put the candle in the candlestick, and wipe the remains of the oil from your fingers upon a piece of clean linen or a tissue — the latter of course is a modern innovation, but a useful one.

Then light the candle, and sit in quiet concentration upon your wish. Above all, *visualize* the thing you want to happen, because if you can make a clear mental picture of it and hold on to that picture, even if only for a few seconds, without doubts or fears or other intervening thoughts, this will have a powerful magical effect. Visualize it symbolically, if you like, so long as the picture is clear.

The burning candle provides the focus for your concentration; but there is no need to stare fixedly at the brightest part of the flame, as this may strain your eyes. Instead, look at the golden glow of the candle as a whole. Appreciate the beauty of the flame, and notice its different colours. Or, if you wish to rest your eyes from its brightness, look at the colour of the candle itself, remembering its symbolic meaning.

Here is a list of colours in which candles can be obtained from any big store, together with their meaning and appropriateness for different rites:

White: psychic development, dispelling of evil influences.

Red: life, vitality, changing your luck for the better.
Blue: healing, spiritual development, occult protection.
Green: fertility, prosperity, gain of money.
Golden yellow: intellectual development, strength of mind.
Pink: love, friendship, happiness.
Purple: occult power, overcoming.
Orange: optimism, success.
Black: revenge, retribution; also, communing with the spirits of the dead.

When buying candles, remember that the more clear and pure their colour is, the better the effect will be.

Burning good quality joss sticks helps the atmosphere of any occult rite; so use some with your candle-burning ritual if you can conveniently do so. The best way to burn joss sticks is the way they do it in the East, where joss sticks originated; that is, get a metal or earthenware bowl, fill it three parts full with sand and stick the joss sticks upright in the sand. Thus, they will not fall over nor drop ash untidily.

When you feel that you have concentrated long enough, take the slip of paper with your wish written on it, and burn it in the flame of the candle, with the thought that you are projecting your wish into the beyond to find fulfilment. Blow out the candle and if it is not consumed you can wrap it up in a piece of clean paper to use again. Remember, however, that you can only use that candle for working again on the same wish. For a different wish you must use a new candle.

Such is the basic lore of candle-burning; and here is a modern witch's charm of thirteen lines, to be used in a candle-burning ceremony:

Candle shining in the night,
With your flame enchanted,
By the powers of magic might,
May my wish be granted.
When the candle sheds its gleam,
At the mystic hour,
Let fulfilment of my dream
Gather secret power.
Flame of magic, brightly burn,
Spirit of the fire.
Let the wheel of fortune turn,

Fire Magic: bringing in the Yule log on Christmas Eve.

Grant me my desire.
One, two, three — so shall it be!

If you are the fortunate possessor of an open fire, here is a brief description of how to interpret the pictures you may see in its glowing coals — or better still, logs. A real old-fashioned log fire, with its wonderful scent, is a splendid thing!

Seat yourself on the rug in front of the fire, with the lights in the room turned low. Throw a handful of kitchen salt on the coals and then wait until the fire is glowing clear. If other people are with you, they must keep silent, as chattering spoils the concentration essential to any real magic.

Much depends on how a particular symbol or picture looks. Is it glowing and cheerful, or dark and sinister? If the thing you see is pleasing, it is a sign of good fortune. But if, for instance, you see a gallows, a skull and crossed bones, or a ruined, broken-down house, these are warnings of danger.

A handsome house or castle, however, is a good sign, especially if it stands upon steps which lead up to it. These show rising prosperity. Trees are a good sign, too; they mean success and happiness. Strangely enough, however, flowers and fruit are not regarded as fortunate when seen in the fire; they mean worries and grief.

Domestic animals, such as cats and dogs, are fortunate if their appearance is friendly. If, however, the animal is snarling or vicious-looking, it means you have an enemy.

Farm animals, such as sheep, are generally lucky, and mean increase of money. A wild animal means news from afar off. A horse means a journey.

To see a ship or an aeroplane also means a journey, probably overseas. Flying birds mean letters on the way. A horseshoe means excellent good luck. A bell means news of a wedding, a cradle means news of a birth, and so on — most omens of this type can be easily interpreted by their natural associations.

If you see a face in the fire, it may remind you of someone you know, or it may be that of a stranger. In either case, if the face is bright and glowing your association with that person will be fortunate; but if the features are dark and shadowy you need to be on your guard.

To see the appearance of an outstretched hand means that someone you know is in trouble and needs help. A dagger or gun means quarrels are threatening. One could not possibly list all the likely symbols here that might be seen; but enough has been said to show the general principles of their interpretation. Two more special fire-symbols may be mentioned. The appearance of a bright, glowing pillar, or pillars upholding an arch, means a love-affair; and a windmill, a wheel, or any turning thing, means change, either for better or worse according to whether it is bright or dark.

Water is a universal symbol of cleansing and regeneration. Sacred rivers, lakes and wells abound in the mysteries of every religion. Springs such as those at Glastonbury and Lourdes have acquired a wonderful reputation for healing powers. This reputation, if enquired into closely, is often found to date back to pre-Christian times.

To see pure spring water bubbling up from the earth is a wonderful and magical thing. People of olden time believed such a spring to have a guardian spirit, to which offerings were made. This is the origin of ceremonies of well-dressing, some of which are still carried out in Britain; and of the custom of throwing coins or pins into wishing-wells and making a wish.

A stream which runs from north to south was anciently believed to have magical properties. So was the place where two streams met. Witches went by the light of the full moon to such a place, in order to carry out their rituals.

As fire is a symbol of the life-force, so water is a symbol of the emotions. Hence the saying that "Still waters run deep". The sun is regarded as the natural ruler of fire, the masculine element; while water, the feminine element, is ruled by the moon. This rulership is evidenced by the tides of the sea, which associate with the phases of the moon.

Witches make use of this symbolism, when they use water for purposes of divination. They take a black bowl filled with water — the old black iron cauldron used to do very well — and drop into it a bright silver coin, an emblem of the moon. Then they gaze through the water at the silver coin, trying to banish all other thoughts until the mind is still and tranquil as the water and psychic visions may appear. This has to be done in a dim light, preferably by candlelight; and the best time for it is when the moon is waxing to the full.

Contrary to popular belief, there is no absolute need for an expensive crystal ball in order to achieve clairvoyant vision. All kinds of things have been used for this purpose; very often bowls or glasses of water. The old-time *kahunas*, or native magicians of Hawaii, used to use a large, smooth, dark-coloured stone, which was placed in a hollowed-out gourd with a little water. When the *kahuna* wanted to use the magic stone to see visions, he simply poured the water over it, so that it was wet and shining, and then gazed at its shiny surface as it lay in the gourd. Such practices as these are nearly as old as mankind itself.

The sounds of a waterfall, or of the waves beating upon the shore, tend to lull the conscious mind into the borderline state of reverie. In this way, the perceptions of the inner mind can rise to the surface, and convey their message to the seer. Natural magicians of all ages have attuned themselves to listen thus to the sounds of nature.

The true poet above all is a natural magician. William Blake, who was deeply interested in the traditions of the Druids, wrote:

> Hear the voice of the Bard!
> Who Present, Past and Future sees;
> Whose ears have heard
> The Holy Word
> That walk'd among the ancient trees . . .

The sigh and rush of the wind is part of the magic of air. Like the beating of waves, it lulls the conscious mind into quietness, and the multitude of thoughts are stilled. Then perception can begin. This may well be the real meaning behind the many sacred groves which were preserved by ancient religions. The Druids had their groves of oak, and so did the goddess Diana at Nemi. The word 'druid' is from the old Welsh *derw-ydd*, meaning 'oak-seer'.

Some sensitive people can attune themselves to the sounds of nature to such an extent that they can actually hear voices and snatches of words, in the rippling stream or the cry of the wind. A seashell, too, can echo a voice to them in this way. Most of us, as children, have held a big hollow shell to our ears and heard in it the sound of the sea. In olden times, a magician would have seemed to hear, not only the echo of the waves, but the voices of the sea-nymphs calling to him.

No doubt the sensitive's own mind supplies the words these voices say; but their message may be a true one, for all that.

Another part of the magic of air is the secret of our breath. The Yogis of the east have made a whole science of various methods of breathing, which would take a book in itself to expound. One of its basic tenets is that the air we breathe contains a vital principle called *prana* and that by the right kind of steady, rhythmic breathing we can recharge our vitality by absorbing more *prana* from the air.

Certainly, we can exist without food or water for some time; but we cannot exist without air, so it must contain very essential principles for sustaining life. To breathe deeply of fresh air will revitalize us, whether we choose to subscribe to the ideas of Yoga or not.

One way to revitalize oneself by rhythmic breathing is to take a walk in the country, or at least somewhere that one does not have to keep dodging traffic. Then time your breathing for an equal time in and out and pausing between each inhalation and exhalation. There is no need to stamp along puffing and blowing, however — this will do no good. Just walk at an easy, natural pace, and let your breath flow gently in and out; but nevertheless breathe deeply and always through the nostrils.

Count one-two-three-four to breathe in, then pause for a count of one-two, and so on. This count is suitable for the average person, though some may like to vary it if their natural rhythm is different. It is the *rhythmic* breath, synchronized with the footsteps, that matters. Do everything in a natural, well-balanced manner, without strain, and the effect will be beneficial both physically and psychically.

Hold the thought that you are drawing vitality from the air and storing it up in your solar plexus — the area just above your navel, which is the body's great storehouse of vital energy. You will find this exercise works best on a fresh, bright sunshiny day. Breathe in the beautiful life that the sun is filling the atmosphere with; breathe out not only physical impurities, but all your worries, doubts, disappointments — let the breeze blow them away. In such simple ways as this you can find the real magic of nature.

The magic of earth is likewise a subject upon which whole books could be and have been written. The goddess of earth has revered in ancient times as the *Magna Mater*, or Great Mother, from whom all things of this physical world are born and to whom all must return, to be regenerated and born again. The chief part of her magic is the lore of herbs, flowers and trees, which will receive a chapter to itself, later on in this book.

We can, however, feel some of the magic of earth by walking or dancing barefoot upon soft grass, and letting the vital, rejuvenating power of earth, oldest of things yet ever young, enter into us. Or we can follow with our eyes the *shapes* of earth — the undulating hills and valleys, the form of some weatherworn, lichen-crusted rock, the way that trees grow upward and spread out in different, harmonious forms of branches. How often do we really *look* at things? When we do, in some quiet spot, we can achieve the same quality of perception by this means, that comes from listening to the wind or the waves. By using our five senses rightly, the inner sixth sense is added to them.

III
Magic of Herbs and Flowers

Herbs and flowers, trees and grasses, mosses, lichens, fungi — all are the wonderful gifts of Mother Earth, and part of her magic. Not only are they beautiful, but all other life on earth is dependent on them. Plants and trees absorb the carbon dioxide which is poisonous to us, and exhale the life-giving oxygen. All life is one; the balance of nature is a very real thing and nothing can be wantonly destroyed without damaging the whole.

Today, people are beginning at last to realize the dangers of allowing this wonderful earth of ours to be ruthlessly ravaged and polluted. The worldly wise, who sneered at people trying to preserve our trees and our countryside and called them 'sentimentalists', are shown to be not so clever after all. Not only does nature need our care; we need the things of nature.

People today have a very high standard of living, compared with what our ancestors used to know. Yet according to the National Association for Mental Health, forty-five per cent of all hospital beds are occupied by people who are mentally ill. What an indictment of our materialistic society!

If people were less 'clever' and more intuitive, if we lived more in harmony with nature, I believe that these terrible statistics could be reduced. True magic, the old wise-craft, is one way of bringing people more in harmony with nature. It teaches its followers not to despise the intellect, but to give it its proper place and no more. It tells us that we are not living truly human lives if we have a very clever brain but a barren heart.

Herbs, flowers and trees are the original sources of medicine for the body and their beauty and subtle influences have always been magical. Old cottage gardens were planted with flowers, not only for their appearance but for their occult properties. Some of these properties are hinted at in the popular names of herbs and flowers — names which in themselves are delightful.

For instance, lad's-love and love-in-a-mist are both plants associated with love spells. The lovely little sea-pink called thrift is a talisman to aid money-saving — it was featured on some issues of the old twelve-sided threepenny piece. The houseleek, which grows on the roofs of old buildings, was called 'Jupiter's Beard' or 'Jupiter's Eye', and it was believed to protect the house from lightning, the weapon of Jupiter the sky-god.

Perhaps it was mere coincidence, but those of us who remember the war will recall how London's bombed sites soon became covered with rose bay willow herb, a tall, waving plant with deep pink flowers, which together with a number of similar plants shares an old, significant name — loosestrife, meaning the ending of war. When the bombers had gone, Nature herself clothed the desolation, not only with one of our most beautiful wild flowers, but one that had a meaning for those who knew the magic of earth.

A plant does not need to be rare in order to be magical. Some of our commonest weeds have fascinating names — for instance, the heads of little yellow flowers called Gold of Pleasure (*Carmelina sativa*), a name instantly evocative of sunlit meadows. Names like bergamot, coriander and rosemary bring to mind the old apothecary's shop, with its jars of pot-pourri and pomanders. Old herbals such as that of John Gerard, published in the seventeenth century, give an amazing variety of names for our native herbs, many of which contain clues to their magical properties.

I am not concerned here so much with the medicinal uses of herbs, as with their subtler, more occult secrets — what one could call green magic. This is sometimes also called floromancy; though strictly speaking the latter word means divination by flowers.

If you would like to bring a breath of the old apothecaries' lore into your home, the pomanders mentioned above are quite easy to make. They consist of a dried orange stuck with cloves, which exhales a spicy fragrance and repels moths from your clothes.

Symbolic magical design showing, in the centre, a symbol of the powers of the Moon. Above is a heart, and below a rose, representing love and life, which are the meanings of the words "amor" and "vita". The garland of twining leaves represents fertility. At the four corners are emblems of the four seasons. Starting at the lower left-hand corner and reading clockwise, they show Spring, Summer, Autumn and Winter.

Get a nice sound orange, with not too thick skin, and a quantity of whole cloves. Then stud the skin of the orange with the cloves until it is completely covered. Some people like to simmer the orange a little in hot water first, to soften it, before sticking in the cloves. Then when the orange has got as many cloves as it will take, so that the whole skin is covered, put it somewhere warm, but not hot, to dry. An airing cupboard, for instance, will answer the purpose very well; and the orange should take about a fortnight to dry. The dried orange can be decorated with coloured ribbon, which will also serve to hang it up, or enclosed in a piece of thin gauze or net and finished off with ribbon. Kept in a dry place, these pomanders will last a long time and retain their fragrance.

Part of old-time village life was the white witch, wise-woman, or herb-wife, with her garden full of fragrant and curious herbs. Probably dwelling in the garden too would be a toad, that village gossip whispered was her familiar. However, the toad's real function in the garden was to keep down insect pests, because insects are the toad's food — he is actually a harmless and intelligent creature and the gardener's friend, in spite of all the sinister legends about him. The wise-woman's garden would probably be far from tidy; but it would be a place of magic, full of scent and colour and mystery.

We too can grow a lucky and magical garden, if we know something of the old plant lore. For instance, we can encourage the sweet-scented things like lavender, rosemary, sage and thyme — the sweet smell of success is not a mere figure of speech; and we can cultivate the plants of the Sun — that is, those which are under the Sun's astrological rulership. The Sun is the giver of life, strength and light. A happy person is said to have a sunny disposition, and this too is the influence brought by the herbs of the Sun in your garden.

Of these, perhaps the most obvious are sunflowers, the real old-fashioned ones as big as a dinner-plate. But if your garden is too small to accommodate these, there is a sovereign magical plant of splendid golden yellow, the hypericum or St John's Wort. This was originally a wild flower, but garden varieties are now obtainable, and if you pick it on Midsummer Day it has magical properties for luck and love, and will drive away evil spirits, according to the old belief. The bright golden-yellow marigolds are flowers of the Sun, too. So is heliotrope, the old name for which is cherry-pie, because that is what it smells like when the hot sun shines on it. The bay-tree, too, is ruled by the Sun, and is another cheerful and healthy influence in your garden.

For money luck, plant the things ruled by Jupiter, the bringer of good fortune and prosperity. Lilac is one of these — and again we notice how sweet-smelling things are luck-bringers. Honeysuckle is another plant of money-luck. The blossoming almond-tree, also ruled by Jupiter, is a beneficent influence as well as being beautiful to look at.

The jolly plants called red-hot-pokers, ruled by Mars, are another pleasant thing to have in your garden. They represent the good side of Mars, life and virility. Most bright red flowers are ruled by Mars, and will give a strengthening influence when mingled with the golden yellow of the solar plants.

The blue morning glory is a lucky garden plant, bringing an influence of peace and happiness. Most bright blue flowers are ruled by Venus, and give aid in matters of love. Forget-me-not, for instance, shows its properties by its name and so does love-in-a-mist. The blue periwinkle has the old name of Sorcerer's Violet, from the belief in its potency as a love charm.

However, the flower of Venus *par excellence* is the rose, in all its varieties, but particularly the pink and red rose, the very emblems of love. The more sweet-scented the rose, the better it is for this purpose; and it is a pity that modern 'progress' has developed roses that are almost scentless, however showy they may be to look at — something rather typical of a good deal of 'progress' itself. Nevertheless, the real old-fashioned roses can still be obtained and they are the ones with the most magical virtue.

Another plant much used in love charms is lemon verbena, which has leaves with a curious sharp perfume. The fragrant myrtle, too, has been sacred to Venus since the days of ancient Greece. The way in which herbs and flowers like this were used to attract love was as follows. They were picked by the light of the full moon, dried, and sewn up into a little sachet made of pale blue or emerald green silk. This was worn next to the skin, either hung round the neck or pinned inside the clothes. Either three, seven or nine of the herbs of Venus were used, and the more fragrant they were, the better.

If you want to have a corner of your garden which is especially magical, plant there the exquisite little flower called Solomon's Seal, with its waxy white blossoms. Plant also the iris, or fleur-de-luce, the 'flower of light', the symbol of inspiration; and, if you can get it, plant the true vervain (*Verbena officinalis*), and the rue or 'Herb of grace'. The last two plants are the favourites of Italian witches, the followers of *La vecchia religione*, the worship of the moon goddess Diana.

Indeed, you cannot possibly have a magical garden unless you have some plants there which honour the moon goddess, the mistress of magic. Most plants with pure white flowers are ruled by the Moon, especially those which give forth their perfume in the evening, like night-scented stock. There are moon-daisies, too, and white narcissi. White lilies are ruled by the Moon and the madonna lily was originally the flower of the moon goddess.

The lore of moon magic, especially in connection with growing things, is almost endless; but its basis is quite simple. The waxing moon is the time of growth and invoking for the things you want. The full moon is the time of integration and perfection, the high tide of psychic matters. The waning moon is the time of decrease and of banishing the things you want to get rid of. The dark of the moon is the time when dark forces are abroad, and not a good period to venture into the psychic realms.

If you wish to have good fortune in the coming month, then on the day of the new moon put some pure white flowers in a vase of silver, crystal or cut glass and stand them in a window where the moonlight can shine on them. They will not only be good to look at, but will attract the beneficent influence of the moon; and if you have grown the flowers youself they will be all the better, because your own loving care and effort has been put into them.

Perhaps, however, you do not have a garden of your own, but can only find room for a few indoor plants, or a window-box. Nevertheless, you can still select some plants with fortunate influences. Geraniums are a fortunate plant for a window-box. The bright red ones have an aura of strength and vitality; they will cheer you up when you are feeling low. The pink ones, especially the rose geranium, which has rose-scented leaves, are lucky for love; while the white ones encourage human fertility and the arrival of babies.

It is possible nowadays to get actual miniature roses to grow as indoor plants, and they have the same rulership by Venus as full-size roses. So if you can get some of these lovely little plants to grow for you, they will bring the beneficent influence of Venus with them, to aid in matters of love, friendship and affection. Another indoor plant of Venus is the delicate maidenhair fern.

Do you want to get things moving and bring an influence of activity and travel to your home? Then the plant for you is the popular indoor grower called *Impatiens*, which is ruled by Mercury. Its colloquial name is Busy Lizzie, which hints at the sort of influence it has, as these old names so often do; and it is a pretty little plant in itself.

Talking of old names for plants, an amusing one is that of the prolific little green creeper, with many tiny leaves, that old cottages often grew in pots on their window-sills outdoors, or just beside the door of the house. It is called Mind-your-own-business — and that is exactly the influence it was supposed to have. It turned aside the inquisitiveness of nosy, gossiping people; and fortunately, this pleasant little evergreen plant is still obtainable.

An evergreen which is not fortunate to grow indoors is ivy, in spite of its popularity for decoration. It is a parasitic plant, and its influence when grown indoors in pots is not a lucky one. "A rare old plant is the ivy green" when clothing some crumbling ruin with its glossy green leaves, or entwined with holly to make a Yuletide garland; but apart from the latter, outdoors is the best place for it.

A better evergreen plant for indoors is the good old-fashioned aspidistra. Being remarkably long-lived, it is ruled by the beneficent side of Saturn; that is, it has Saturn's good qualities of tranquillity and endurance. This rulership is typified by the fact that the aspidistra has come to be the very epitome of Victorian respectability and homely comfort. Well, there is a good deal to be said for homely comfort; and the aspidistra's influence is to calm and dispel fears, especially those which oppress us by night and bring bad dreams. When properly looked after, its dark green leaves should have a sheen on them which makes it a handsome plant.

Another pot plant to ward off bad dreams is the cyclamen. People grew it in their houses in olden times because they believed it kept away evil spirits.

A lucky indoor collection of plants would be one for each day of the week, according to their planetary rulerships. The Sun rules Sunday, the Moon, Monday; Mars, Tuesday; Mercury, Wednesday; Jupiter, Thursday; Venus, Friday and Saturn, Saturday. So you could have a bright orange flower for Sunday, a white one for Monday, a red one for Tuesday, a yellow one, or a Busy Lizzie, for Wednesday, a purple one for Thursday, a light blue one or a miniature rose for Friday and an evergreen for Saturday.

If you want to bring good vibrations to your home, get two vases of bright golden-yellow or orange-coloured flowers, full of the cheerful influence of the Sun. Place them on opposite sides of the living room, and arrange a mirror behind each vase, so that the mirrors reflect the vases and each other. This will give an invisible ray of solar influence across your room, which will serve to dispel evil and encourage good, so long as the flowers remain fresh and alive. (Never keep cut flowers that have started to wilt and decay, as their influence then is not a beneficial one). You can also perform this piece of flower magic with any other flowers whose planetary influence you wish to invoke.

If you are feeling low and depressed, perhaps after an illness, for instance, a vase full of thistles in your room will give you an influence of restored strength and vitality. Thistles have always been esteemed for their health-giving properties, and were much used medicinally in olden times, especially the large variety called milk thistle, which was known as *Carduus benedictus*, 'blessed thistle'. Some big, handsome varieties of thistle make good garden plants, too, and their presence was anciently supposed to ward off thieves.

The silvery dried seed pods of honesty (*Lunaria biennis*) are fortunate to have as a decoration in your home. They bring money luck; their Latin name shows that they are ruled by the

Moon, and they remind one of the Moon's metal, silver. 'Honest effort well rewarded' is the meaning of this plant.

The magical virtues of herbs and flowers is a subject one could write about almost indefinitely; but we must find room here to talk about trees. Did you know, for instance, that the elder is a witches' tree, and that it is asking for trouble to cut down or prune one without seeking leave of the tree spirit that dwells invisibly within? Or that the oak tree, the ash and the thorn are called 'the fairy triad', because where they are found growing together you stand a good chance of seeing the fairies — if you have the second sight, that is?

Trees are things that have a personality of their own; they can be friendly or otherwise. The elm is traditionally an unfriendly tree to mankind, beautiful though the traceries of its branches are against a winter sky. Out in the broad meadows is the place for it, rather than too near your home. But the apple tree, with its pink blossom and kindly fruit, is one of the friendliest trees there are.

If you know anyone who is pruning or cutting down an old apple tree, ask for some of its wood to make a luck-bringing fire for your home. Soak the logs of apple-wood in sea-water or brine for twenty-eight days — a lunar month. Then dry them out thoroughly and burn them on your fire. They will not only delight you with their many-coloured flames and the sweet smell they make while burning. Within a month, says the old story, some good luck will come to your door.

Other fortunate trees to have near your home are the graceful silver birch, the maple tree which is a harbinger of prosperity and the grand old guardian oak. The holly tree is a good neighbour, too, and brings money luck; but the plane tree growing near one's house is supposed to do just the reverse and is sometimes known as the tree of poverty.

Those strange trees called monkey-puzzles are not regarded as fortunate; they are believed to be bringers of discord. Presumably, they get their name because it would puzzle a monkey how to climb such a spiky thing; and their spikiness, by reason of the old doctrine of signatures or like producing like, made old-time wise-women look on them with disfavour.

The ash is a beneficent tree and often mentioned in old spells and legends. For instance, one old book of spells tells of

The Woodland Path

invoking the aid of the ash tree to charm warts. Cross each wart with a pin three times, and after each crossing repeat, "Ash tree, ashen tree, pray buy this wart of me." Then stick the pin in the tree and, by and by, the wart will disappear and grow on the tree instead. But you must do this secretly and not tell anyone about it, or the spell will not work. The best time to do this is in the waning of the moon — and use new pins, a different one for each wart. Today, doctors and psychologists accept that warts *can* be charmed, though they do not know just how the old magic works. But why worry, so long as it does?

An even ash-leaf — that is, one with an even number of leaflets on it — is as lucky a thing as a four-leafed clover, according to ancient lore. It was particularly valued as a love-charm and if you put it under your pillow you would dream of your true love. One old rhyme, that country maidens said when they found an even ash-leaf, ran as follows:

> This even ash I double in three,
> The first man I meet my true love shall be;
> If he be married let him pass by,
> But if he be single, let him draw nigh.

Of course, the essence of the charm was for the one who worked it to hide the ash-leaf in her bosom at some time and place where the next man she met was likely to be the one she wanted.

Trees as large as the ash, however, are seldom found in people's gardens today; but a smaller tree, and one replete with good magic since the days of the Druids, is the rowan or mountain ash. Its bright red berries are a splendid sight in the autumn and no evil spirits can abide it, nor black magic flourish in its presence. Birds love its fruit, and this should not be grudged to them; because to have plenty of wild birds frequenting your garden is a sign of a good atmosphere in that place. Places of ill omen are those where no birds sing.

The magical lore and legend of trees, like that of herbs, is almost endless. Only a glimpse has been given here into the realms of green magic; but enough, I hope, to awaken deeper interest in enjoying and caring for the wondrous bounties of Earth, the Great Mother.

IV
Magic of Numbers

A great deal has been written about numerology, or the magical use of numbers; but much of it is so contradictory that the student is left bewildered. One reason for this is that numerologists approach the subject in various different ways. Some use the kabbalistic numerical equivalents of the Hebrew alphabet and try to adapt these to the English alphabet, for the purpose of working out the numerical value of people's names. Others base their conclusions upon the numbers derived from the mysterious Tarot cards. Still others seek to relate numbers to astrology and interpret a number according to its supposed planetary correspondence.

Perhaps a good deal of this muddle can be straightened out, if we remember that numerology is primarily about *numbers* and only in a related sense about astrology or the Tarot. We may equate 1 with the Sun, 2 with the Moon, and so on; but this will only be true in relation to our little planet. This will be one case of the meaning of the numbers 1 and 2, so to speak, taken in relation to our small, local corner of this galaxy; whereas the principles of mathematics will apply throughout the universe. There would still be unity and duality if our planet and our solar system had ceased to exist.

Considering this, we realize the depth and immensity of the study of numbers. It is something which drew the attention of the most renowned philosophers of the past, notably Pythagoras and Plato; and yet a child can sum it up by counting on his fingers. The signs for numbers are known as digits from the Latin *digitus*, a finger.

Numerologists generally get at the essence of a number by reducing it to a single digit. They do this by adding the figures of a number together until only one digit is left. For instance,

527 would be added as 5 + 2 + 7 = 14, and then further reduced to 1 + 4 = 5. It is a curious fact that if you take the final resulting digit of such an addition away from the original number, the result will always be divisible by 9. Thus 527 − 5 = 522, and 522 divides by 9 to make 58. So the sum of the digits of a number is, in a sense, the root of that number, and the process is not as illogical as it looks. Any number above 9 consists of the sum of its digits plus a certain number of nines.

The number from 1 to 9, with the addition of the cipher 0, are the basis of all mathematics, and these are the numbers which numerologists usually work with, reducing all larger numbers to a single digit as above. An old attribution of these numbers, which dates back at least to the sixteenth century and may be much older,* gives them astrological correspondences as follows: the Sun, 1 and 4; the Moon, 2 and 7; Jupiter, 3; Mercury, 5; Venus, 6; Saturn, 8; and Mars, 9. The Sun and the Moon, being luminaries, have two numbers each. 1 is the positive number of the Sun, and 4 the negative; 7 is the positive number of the Moon, and 2 the negative.

This table will, I think, be found a help in interpreting the meaning of numbers; but it should be kept in mind that it is the properties of each number which matter in this study and these astrological correspondences are only likenesses and approximations.

The idea of reducing a person's name to its numerical equivalent is a very old one indeed. In the Hebrew, the Greek and the Arabic alphabets, the letters all have a numerical equivalent and the occult properties of numbers and letters are the basis of much mystical lore among the people who have used these alphabets since ancient times. Some numerologists today, as mentioned above, use a number code based upon the ancient Hebrew, in order to interpret names; but the big difficulty involved in using such a code is that the Hebrew alphabet was designed for writing the Hebrew language, not modern English, and a precise correspondence between it and the English alphabet is not possible. The same applies to Greek and Arabic; each alphabet was designed for

***De Occulta Philosophia*, Cornelius Agrippa, 1531.

writing its own language and no other. The result is, that of all the numerologists who use codes based on the Hebrew, one can scarcely find two whose codes are precisely the same and this leads to endless uncertainty.

It seems more logical to me, therefore, to emulate those numerologists who take the *principle* of the old kabbalistic alphabets and apply it to modern English, instead of trying to equate the English alphabet with Hebrew and filling the gaps with the aid of Greek.

This is the code I propose to use, and it has at least the virtue of being simple and without variation, while still based upon ancient ideas.

1	2	3	4	5	6	7	8	9
A	B	C	D	E	F	G	H	I
J	K	L	M	N	O	P	Q	R
S	T	U	V	W	X	Y	Z	

The numerical equivalent of each letter is shown by the number it falls under. So if you want to see what number your name gives, just write down the letters of the name you are most generally known by, put the numerical equivalent under each, add the numbers together and add the digits again as described before, until you have just one digit remaining. That will be the number of your name and it will tell you what the influence of that name is. You will probably find that it gives you a good idea of your personality, as reflected by that name.

Remember that names can be changed, and so can personality. This is why the latter term is derived from *persona*, a Latin word meaning a mask, as used by players on a stage.

The meanings of the numbers from 1 to 9 may be briefly summarised as follows:

1: this is the vibration of the leader. A forthright person, dominant and active. Strong-willed, too, and can be self-centred; but with plenty of initiative and originality. The number of the pioneer.

2: a much gentler influence than that of the foregoing. One who values friendship and sentiment. Sometimes shy and lacking in resolution. Fond of home life and domestic happiness. Often gifted with psychic powers, especially mediumship.

3: a lucky number and often happy-go-lucky, giving a cheerful, rather bohemian influence. Generous and optimistic. Sometimes self-indulgent and extravagant. People who take a sporting attitude to life.

4: a fine, four-square influence, steady and reliable. Loyal and hard-working; but can be rather stubborn and unimaginative. Practical, persistent, and matter-of-fact.

5: an active and rather changeable influence, giving its subjects many different talents and interests. Unusual powers of mind, but often marred by impatience. Fond of travel, and dislike to be tied down.

6: the number of harmony and beauty. Its subjects are cultured and artistic. Fond of luxury, sympathetic and peace-loving.

7: the mystic number. Its subjects are idealistic and often misunderstood. Thoughtful and self-possessed, they can become 'loners'; but they have reserves of inner strength. Sometimes psychic and intuitive.

8: the number of organization and material power. Conservative, sometimes stern and pessimistic; but solid, strong and high-principled. Cautious and careful.

9: a number of great strength, for good or ill. Active, courageous and ambitious; but can be jealous and over-hasty. High-spirited and fond of excitement.

The above could be described as thumb-nail sketches of the influence of each number, as seen when it works out as the number of your name. One should remember that everyone has the faults of their virtues — and the virtues of their faults! For instance, a 2 personality may seem demure and self-effacing in comparison with more dashing types; but would be a wonderful home-maker and may be much pleasanter to live with. A 9 person may be jealous and rather domineering; but he will stand by you and fight for you through thick and thin. A 4 may seem a plodder and an old square; but what a truthful and trustworthy person he is to fall back on, when some of the more brilliant ones have let you down.

If we really want to change our personality, then changing our name may be one way to do it. The deliberate adoption of a new name is, after all, something that people do because they want to make a change in their life. They are, for some reason, dissatisfied with their previous name. Subconsciously, perhaps, there is some part of their being that they are striving to express, and they choose a name that will enable them to do this. Sometimes, indeed, a change of name does make a striking difference to a person's life. If we read the biographies of people who have in some way made an impact on the world, it is surprising to find how many of them have changed the name they were given at birth.

For instance, who ever heard of Edward Alexander Crowley? But the flamboyant Aleister Crowley became a legend in his lifetime. Greta Gustafsson was just another Swedish girl trying to get into films. Then she changed her name to Greta Garbo. Adolf Hitler's family originally went under the name of Schickelgruber. Can you imagine people shouting "*Heil* Schickelgruber"?

Curiously enough, the name Adolf Hitler adds to 2 — that supposedly gentle, self-effacing number! Was Hitler a medium, who became the tool and instrument of sinister powers? The town where he was born, Branau-am-Inn, was noted as the birthplace of a number of well-known mediums. We know that he was fascinated by the occult, and that it played a big part in his life. Numerology can often given unexpected insights like this into life and character.

What, however, is the real number of a person's destiny? We read so much in different books, of lucky numbers, fatidic numbers and so on; but one thing is certain. We may change the number our name makes as often as we like; but there is one number we cannot change, because fate decided that for us — the number of our birthdate. It seems logical, therefore, to select this as representing the number of our life's destiny, rather than the more ephemeral name-number, which shows the personality we display to the world. The destiny number is something deeper. Occultists who believe in reincarnation tell us that the birthdate number represents the lesson we have come to earth to learn in this lifetime.

We arrive at the birthdate number by writing down the figures of our date of birth, and then adding them together until only one digit is left. Thus, if you were born on July 18th, 1941, you write down 18.7.1941, which adds to 31, giving a final digit of 4; so 4 is your number of destiny. The process is very simple and the numbers are interpretated according to the general ideas of their meaning already given, though in a rather deeper sense.

Perhaps we can understand them better if we consider the implications of each number as the sequence unfolds. First, we have the number one, the potential germ or seed, the unit of evolving life. It represents man seeking to establish himself as an individual. Then comes the number, two, not merely two ones but two complementary opposites — man and woman, light and darkness, fire and water, all the pairs of opposites without which manifested life could not exist. Two represents the stage at which man realizes there are other people in the world besides himself. But two opposites cannot accomplish anything unless they are united, any more than two straight lines can enclose a space.

With the number three, however, we have the triangle, the first geometrical figure. The opposites are united, and life has begun to expand. The number three is a sacred, magical and lucky number, and has been throughout the ages, because it represents the manifestation of life in this way. One typical example of its sacredness is the trinity worshipped in ancient Egypt: Isis, Osiris and Horus, the Mother, Father and Son.

The number four represents the foursquare foundation of the world, the four elements, the four cardinal points, the four winds, and so on. It typifies law, orderliness, and regularity — morning, noon, evening and night; childhood, youth, maturity and old age; and so on. But this very orderliness needs to be enlivened by something more, and so we progress to the number five.

Five is the number of mind, the human being seeking experience through the five senses. With the number five, man seeks to look beyond the world of the four elements, to be untrammelled by his surroundings, to travel and progress.

By using his mind, man is led onwards to the number six, the number of beauty and harmony. Culture and artistry enter into his life. He appreciates the finer things; but he still seeks beyond. Gracious living in itself is not enough. He advances to the meaning of number seven, the mystic number, which teaches him to look inwards and know himself, to seek for the inner light within his own soul.

But mysticism and idealism need to be brought into the realms of practical reality. So man also needs the number eight, the number of organization, by which ideals and ideas can be crystallized into form, to make a better life. Even so, such forms cannot endure for ever; and so the number nine, powerful and regenerative, eventually comes into man's life, sometimes destroying, but also clearing the ground so that life can renew itself eternally.

These nine digits, together with the nought, the circle which represents infinity and eternity, make possible all the calculations of mathematics. No wonder that the ancient occult philosophers held numbers to be sacred, and representative of divine things.

We may put this knowledge to practical use by considering the life-lesson to be derived from each number of destiny, as indicated by the birthdate:

One: this teaches us to be self-reliant, and to develop ourselves as individuals.

Two: this teaches the need for co-operation with others, and to cultivate sympathy and understanding.

Three: this teaches the expansion of consciousness, generosity and optimism.

Four: this teaches orderliness, firmness and the need to build upon a foundation of truth.

Five: this teaches the search for knowledge and wisdom, and the need to find freedom from limitations.

Six: this teaches the appreciation of beauty, and the finding of harmony with oneself and others.

Seven: this teaches the way of withdrawal into one's own soul, and the finding of inner peace and enlightenment.

Eight: this teaches organization, and the ability to use material power wisely and with justice.

Nine: this teaches truly creative living, and the right use of strength and initiative.

If we look out for the occurrence of our name-numbers and birthdate-numbers in our lives, we shall find them, or numbers whose digits reduce to them, turning up in all sorts of places. But which one of these numbers can be considered our lucky number?

The old belief is that odd numbers are more lucky than even ones. The Roman poet Virgil tells us that "the gods delight in odd numbers". The reason for this is that odd numbers were regarded as positive and pertaining to spiritual things, while even numbers were negative, and pertaining to material things. Hence, it may be a good idea to choose as your lucky number that one of your numbers which is odd. If they are both odd, choose the one which appeals to you most. Experience will soon show you which is your best choice.

If your numbers include 2 and 4, remember that these numbers have a sympathetic connection with 7 and 1 respectively, because of their astrological correspondences, as set out earlier in this chapter. So if your number as given by name or birthdate is 2, then 7 could be lucky for you; and if it is 4, then 1 could be your lucky number.

6 is a fortunate number, because of its associations with harmony and perfection. 8 is not generally considered fortunate; but if both your name and your birthdate give this number, then it is evidently so strongly connected with your life that it may be fortunate for you. Try it and see; but if your life seems fatally involved with eights in an unfortunate way, remember you can always change your name to one that adds to a different number.

Alternatively, some numerologists regard the day of the month on which one was born as giving one's lucky number, reducing it if necessary to a single digit as before. It seems to me to be a weaker influence in one's life, however, than either the name or the birthdate number. But if, as often happens, this number is the same as either the name or the total birthdate number, then it reinforces the strength of that number in one's life; and if it seems to give a more fortunate vibration than either of these two numbers, then adopting it as one's lucky number would certainly seem a good idea.

When you have decided which is your lucky number, which the foregoing information should help you to do, then look out for it in your daily life. Watch for telephone numbers and house numbers; notice days and times; add up people's names — almost everything has a number connected with it in some way. Keep a notebook and record things that have proved fortunate or otherwise, from a numerological point of view. Numerology can be a fascinating hobby, as well as a practical means of help and guidance.

A further note needs to be made about the numbers 4 and 7. When Cornelius Agrippa recorded their astrological correspondences in the sixteenth century, only the *visible* heavenly bodies of our solar system were regarded by astrologers; that is, Saturn, Jupiter, Mars, Venus, Mercury, and the Sun and Moon. However, since that time other planets have been discovered and named Uranus, Neptune and Pluto.

Astrologers have had time to assess the influences of Uranus and Neptune and data is being accumulated about Pluto, although its influence at the moment remains as dark and obscure as this remote planet itself. These planets are sometimes regarded as being of a more spiritual and esoteric nature than the visible planets. Only as man has progressed along the road of his development has he become aware of them. (Although there is some evidence that the ancients knew a great deal more about science and astronomy than they have hitherto been credited with; see *We Are Not the First*, by Andrew Tomas, Sphere Books, London, 1972).

Some numerologists have ascribed the influence of Uranus to the number 4 and that of Neptune to the number 7. When one is dealing with the more spiritually-advanced type of person, I think this inference is well-based. However, one must use one's own judgment, from practical observation.

The influence of Uranus is unconventional, revolutionary and even eccentric and 'cranky' if carried to excess. It gives intellectual brilliance and inventiveness. In material matters, it is connected with aviation and space-travel.

The influence of Neptune is mystical and visionary. It is often connected with strong psychic powers; but if carried to excess, it can be the passport to a world of beautiful illusion. In material matters, it rules, among other things, hallucinogenic drugs, typical of a condition of highly-coloured and delusive fantasy.

As with all other planets and signs, both Uranus and Neptune have their good and their bad sides — or perhaps one should say rather, their positive and their negative sides. Occultists who watch the trends in human history have observed that the discovery of Uranus in 1781 was the precursor of the French Revolution and that of Neptune in 1846 was the precursor of Spiritualism. These tides in human thought have had widespread influence and each was typical of the planet whose discovery preceded it.

V

Magic of Colours

Why do some people so delight to surround themselves with drab, depressing colours? There is no need of it these days, now that we have emerged from the era when 'good taste' was synonymous with dullness. Moreover, there is much more in colour than people think. It is not a mere decoration. Each colour is a vibration, with an effect that may be beneficial or otherwise.

Pure, clear colour is an uplifting influence. We can see this in the glorious colours of nature, the green of sunlit grass, the blue of the sky, the soft, glowing hue of a deep red rose, or the subtle shades of purple on distant hills. And what a variety of colours can be seen on the sea — jade greens, translucent blues, delicate purples and violets and the strange, sinister greys of the impending storm. Then, at sunset and at dawn, everything is again transformed by rosy fire and burning gold. With these wonderful colours all around us, we should never dress in dreary or inharmonious shades, or have ugliness in our home surroundings, however simple the latter may be.

In fact, artistic simplicity is much preferable to lavish bad taste. There can be expensive ugliness and dreariness, as well as that which results from poverty. But the home of a person who has true magic in them, whether they be rich or poor, will have a kind of subtle atmosphere, an intriguing attractiveness — even if it is not very tidy!

The old time witches, of course, knew all about this question of atmosphere. The cottage of the village witch, or the magician's house in the side-street of some quaint old town, would be deliberately adorned with such objects as would strike the imagination of a visitor and put them in the right mood for a magical consultation. The smell of old leather-bound books and parchments mingled with that of jars of spices and bunches of drying herbs; the sight of strange objects, half-hidden, half-displayed — such as, for instance, a stuffed alligator hanging from the ceiling, or a skull upon a shelf in some dark corner, while shining silver witch-balls reflected the flame of a scented candle; all these things were deliberately used to act as suggestions to the mind. And in the days when all classes believed implicitly in magic, their effect must have been potent.

In these more sophisticated times, such a display might seem merely theatrical. Nevertheless, the effect of deliberately created atmosphere is not to be despised; only the present day magician sets about it in a less crude way than our ancestors did.

Soft lighting, for instance, is more pleasing and conducive to meditation than a bright overhead light. Certain colours have a soothing effect; others are warming and exciting. This, indeed, is a fundamental principle of the use of colour. We can divide colours, in a sense, into masculine and feminine.

The masculine colours are those which have a warming, stimulating effect — the fiery tones of red and orange, while the calming and soothing colours are the shades of blue and green. Yellow holds a midway place between the two; while the shades of purple are mysterious, and often favoured by those interested in the occult.

It will be seen how the three primary colours, red, blue and yellow, demonstrate what occultists call the Law of the Triangle, the two opposites with the uniting and harmonizing principle between them. Red is the active, stimulating colour; blue is the passive, soothing colour; while yellow holds the balance of harmony between the two.

Magicians of olden time regarded red as the colour of life, probably because of the redness of blood. Hence they often used red ink to inscribe magical sigils, in order to give them symbolic life. This idea goes back a very long way into human history. Men of the Stone Age used to cover the bones of their dead with red ochre, presumably in order to give them a new life. Our great-grandparents put their faith in red flannel underwear to protect them from colds and chills; and the fact that the flannel had to be red was, whether they realized it or not, a remnant of a lingering belief in red as a magical colour.

Too much red in one's surroundings, however, can be over-stimulating to the nerves and make one irritable. Soft, rosy reds are more gentle in their effect, more subtly warming, than the bright scarlets and vermilions.

While red is the colour that stimulates the physical body, orange stimulates the more subtle forces. It is the colour of the sun, the source of vitality, as well as of light and heat. Upon the glorious golden sun, the life of our solar system of planets depends.

We see before us the countryside on a grey day. The landscape looks dull and lifeless. Then the sun comes out and immediately there is a wonderful transformation. All at once, the colours seem brighter. The air has a new freshness. The water sparkles with diamond drops. No wonder the ancient pagans worshipped the sun as the symbol of the divine source of life.

> Thy dawning is beautiful in the horizon of heaven,
> O living Aton, beginning of life!
> When thou risest in the eastern horizon of heaven,
> Thou fillest every land with thy beauty;
> For thou art beautiful, great, glittering, high over the earth;
> Thy rays, they encompass the lands, even all thou hast made.
> Thou art Ra, and thou hast carried them all away captive;
> Thou bindest them by thy love.
> Though thou art afar, thy rays are on the earth;
> Though thou art on high, thy footprints are the day.

So sang Akhenaton (Amenhotep IV), who was Pharaoh of Egypt over three thousand years ago. Still today, the orange ray will help to restore vitality and will-power to those who feel weak and depleted. Wear the colour when you can in your clothing and use it in the furnishing of your surroundings. If it seems too strong a colour, however, to be used like this — though thank goodness even men today are beginning to overcome the convention of drabness — then get a piece of orange-coloured material, preferably silk, and wear it around the middle of your body, next to the skin. This method can be used for any colour whose vibration you wish to attune yourself to.

The colour yellow is a sunshine colour also, and

particularly stimulates the mind. The Buddhist monks of the East, some of the most deeply contemplative of men, wear yellow robes. Those sensitive enough to be able to see the colours of the human aura, have often testified to the nimbus of golden light which surrounds the head of a person whose mind is highly evolved. This is the origin of the halo, which has become the artistic convention for depicting saints or spiritual beings.

Green is the predominant colour of nature and its influence is restful and calming. For this reason, hospitals have adopted it in recent years for the garb of surgeons and the staff of operating theatres. Yet some people fear green as an 'unlucky' colour. This feeling is a lingering relic of the belief that green is the colour of the fairies. In Sir Walter Scott's poem, "The Lady of the Lake", he refers to "The fairies' fatal green" and he explains this in a note to the poem, as follows: "As the Daoine Shi or Men of Peace — i.e., fairies — wore green habits they were supposed to take offence when any mortals ventured to assume their favourite colour."

However, people who love nature and are sensitive to the unseen often show a liking for green in their clothes and surroundings; and for them, green is not unlucky, because they have a natural affinity for it. To the occult philosophers of old, green had a spiritual meaning. It signified the secret immanence of the divine spirit in the life of all things. They had a mystical saying in Latin, *Linea viridis gyrat universa*, which is explained by a passage in the writings of Thomas Vaughan (1621-1666):

"It compasseth the heavens and in them the earth, like a green rainbow or one vast sphere of viridity, and from this viridity the divine influences are showered down like rain, through the ether, into the globes of the fixed stars."

Vaughan's book, *Lumen de Lumine*, is an account of a mystical dream, in which he journeys to a waste and desolate land. This strange country of the mind is brought to life when the goddess of nature appears, "attired in thin loose silk but so green that I never saw the like, for the colour was not earthly."

There are many people today who need this redemption of nature. Modern so-called 'civilization' has forced them to lead frustrated, unnatural lives, cut off from the true sources of vitality and happiness, which are to be found in nature. The real joy of living is not to be bought with money, or found in so-called 'getting on in the world' or 'being a success', as many who have spent their lives in pursuit of these things have learned to their cost.

To see the sunlight through the green leaves of a forest in summer, or to walk upon the turf of green hills, to rest the mind from thinking intellectually and just feel intuitively, this is medicine for body and soul. There is plenty of green available for us in nature; the vibration of the green ray is there in every leaf, in every blade of grass, if we will but attune ourselves to it.

Nature has given generously, also, of the spiritual and healing colour, blue, in the great expanse of the sky. Wilhelm Reich, the famous psychologist, believed that all nature is permeated with a subtle energy which he called 'orgone', because it is the energy which is present in the sexual climax, or orgasm — the basic energy of life itself. The prevailing colour of this energy, according to Reich, is blue-violet and it is this energy, permeating the atmosphere, which gives its glorious colour to the sky.

Whether or not we accept Reich's ideas, it is a fact that spiritual healers make much use of blue and healing sanctuaries are often hung with drapes of this colour. In the East, clear bright blue is believed to be a protection against black magic and the evil eye; and necklaces containing bright blue beads are often worn for this purpose.

Blue is the colour of the symbolic garter bestowed by the Order of the Garter, Britain's senior order of chivalry; it is also used in the Masonic tradition, where it signifies fidelity, friendship and universal sympathy. The three degrees of Craft Masonry are sometimes called 'Blue Masonry', because of the prevalence of the colour blue in their regalia. Blue is both literally and symbolically a heavenly colour.

One way in which the benefits of the blue ray can be attuned to is by using light which has filtered through blue glass. Glass has always taken the colour blue with particular richness and deepness. Antique Bristol glass has long been famous for its wonderful blue colour; but much less expensive glass than this can be bought which comes in beautiful shades of blue. If, then, one can obtain a stoppered bottle or decanter of richly-coloured blue glass, it can be used to get the benefit of this healing colour. Fill the bottle with water and stand it in a sunlit place for a couple of days. To drink this water will be beneficial to health and psychic sensitivity.

Alternatively, get a piece of deep blue glass and frame it so that the sharp edges are covered. Hold this glass so that the sun shines through it and the coloured ray is directed upon any part of the body affected by illness, preferably upon the bare skin. Do this for as long as you conveniently can, up to about half-an-hour at a time. Many beneficial results have been claimed from this practice. Electric light is sometimes used to shine through the glass; but warm natural sunlight is best, if available.

Indigo and violet are closely akin to blue; the latter colour in fact shades into them. The glorious amethyst violet is a colour connected with mysticism and deeply religious feeling; yet it is also a sensual colour, emphasizing the deep psychological connection between the instincts of religion and those of sex. Aleister Crowley said of it that it is "a vibration which is at the same time spiritual and erotic". It is a colour of richness, royalty and opulence.

Indigo is the colour of the midnight deeps of space; making one think of the beyond, of infinity. It is the colour of things tremendous and remote and hence up to now has been little used on its own for magical purposes.

The attribution of the seven rainbow or prismatic colours to the seven visible heavenly bodies of our solar system, according to astrology, is as follows (this is the attribution of western magic, as given by the famous Order of the Golden Dawn):

Red: Mars.
Orange: Sun.
Yellow: Mercury.
Green: Venus.
Blue: Moon.
Indigo: Saturn.
Violet: Jupiter.

According to the teachings of the same occult fraternity, the rainbow colours were shaded through the signs of the Zodiac as follows:

The Bewitchments of Love and Hate

Aries: Scarlet.
Taurus: Red-orange.
Gemini: Orange.
Cancer: Amber.
Leo:Yellow, greenish.
Virgo: Green, yellowish.
Libra: Emerald green.
Scorpio: Green-blue.
Sagittarius: Blue.
Capricorn: Indigo.
Aquarius: Violet.
Pisces: Crimson.

These attributions can act as a guide for those who wish to cultivate the powers of their particular sign or planet. It should be remembered that colours can always be modified and harmonized by the skilful juxtaposition of other shades; or enlivened by a touch of contrasting colour. Only experience can teach one to do this and achieve a pleasing effect; but experimenting with colours is a fascinating and truly magical thing, because colour knowledge played an important part in ancient magic.

As you become more sensitive to colour, you will be able to use it in specifically magical ways. One of these is the visualizing of colours in the aura, for purposes of strengthening and protection.

The aura has been called "the human atmosphere". It is a field of force surrounding the human body, in which clairvoyant sensitives can see many different colours, according to the mental and emotional state of the person. The more clear and beautiful the colours of the aura, the more spiritually evolved the person is. The general shape of the aura is like that of an egg, as it radiates from the human body in all directions, extending outwards for a distance of some two or three feet, though in exceptional cases it may be more.

People are seldom able to see the aura today, largely because they have been conditioned not to believe in such things and taught that it is 'all imagination'; or worse still, frightened by tales that 'all that sort of thing is of the devil — and fear acts as a barrier to the free use of our natural innate powers. However, if one can view the naked human body in a dim light, against a dark background, with practice and perseverance one can learn to see the aura.

We are often conscious of the influence of other people's auras, whether we can see them or not. They account for our instinctive likes and dislikes when meeting others, according to whether their aura harmonizes with our own or otherwise.

By visualizing a colour and picturing it mentally as surrounding us and filling our aura with its particular radiance and beauty, we can attune ourselves to the beneficial effects of that colour. Certain colours especially, are valuable for protecting us against various undesirable vibrations.

The clear, rosy reds will give us an influence of strength and confidence, when in the presence of lowering conditions, such as the danger of infection from illness, or the depleting effect that sick people sometimes have on others. Think of the glorious hues of red roses, and let their colour fill your aura, if you have to go somewhere on a miserable wintry day, for instance, where people are coughing and sneezing and everything looks depressing. The red ray will help to warm and protect you. I remember once using this method to make more bearable a wretched winter train journey in an unheated carriage and I suffered no cold or chill from the trip.

If you want protection for the mind, however, choose golden yellow. Charge your aura with this colour when you have to enter the presence of people who will try to overcome you in argument. Do this, and keep a positive mental attitude and their plausible tongues will be less able to talk you into something you may later regret. Golden yellow is the colour of highly developed intellect, and it will brighten your reasoning powers, especially if you picture it as a shining nimbus around your neck, repelling insidious arguments and suggestions.

Sometimes even more insidious, however, is the danger which attacks us through our emotions. The auric colour which will cool our emotional reactions and transmute them to a higher vibration, is the clear, bright, spiritual blue. When we are in danger of losing control of ourselves, we are said to 'see red'. These old sayings often have a good deal of instinctive truth — though of course it is the impure shades of auric colour that are referred to when we speak of going green with envy, being yellow in the sense of cowardice, or depressed because we have got the blues. Dark, muddy blues really are the colours of depression, as sickly greens and yellows are of envy and cowardice, and harsh, glaring scarlet that of rage. The purer and more beautiful a colour is, the better is its influence; and the pure and beautiful blue will help us to rise above the lower types of emotion, if we will remember it and visualize it when we are tempted to give way to them. There is a great deal of nonsense talked about black magic; but nevertheless, black magic does exist. It is probably unlikely that you will ever be brought into contact with real disembodied evil, as most so-called black magicians have no power except to instil fear by the use of threats, working on their victim's imagination. However, it is possible that at some time you may encounter a genuine evil influence; and you can protect yourself against it by concentrating upon the clear and shining white light, the divine white brilliance, which is the symbol of the highest spiritual power we mortals can visualize.

Picture this light as surrounding you with a shining aura of protection, which overcomes everything lower than itself. See it as the most brilliant and pure whiteness of the spirit, in which you take refuge. An aura which is strengthened in this way will repel evil and cause it to rebound upon the sender, if the influence has been deliberately launched against you. Once you have aspired towards the higher plane and made contact with its vibrations, the presence of the white light in your aura will cast out fear.

VI
Magic of Talismans and Amulets

The wearing of talismans and amulets was practised by all the great civilizations of the past and especially that of ancient Egypt, from which so many of the basic ideas of magic derive. Nor has their popularity waned today. A host of so-called 'lucky charms' may be seen advertised for sale, while jewellers display in their windows attractive pendants and rings of a more or less magical nature. These often feature 'birth-stones' according to the sign of the Zodiac one was born under.

Is there really any truth in the beliefs behind these legendary luck-bringers? Can a person really attract good luck, or avert misfortune, by wearing such things? Centuries of magical faith and experience, at any rate, support such beliefs. The form of many traditional amulets, such as the ankh cross and the swastika, goes back to a vast antiquity; and so does the belief in the occult virtues of precious stones.

There is an essential difference between a talisman and an amulet, although the two words are often regarded as meaning more or less the same thing. A talisman is believed to have some occult potency for attracting some benefit to its possessor; while an amulet wards off danger and misfortune.

Magicians throughout the ages have made and consecrated talismans for some particular purpose and old books of magic are full of designs and instructions for making talismans. Sometimes a powerful talisman was believed to be capable of both attracting good luck and repelling evil; but an amulet has always been an occult protection, especially against the dreaded power of the evil eye.

Precious stones have been used both as amulets and talismans. Apart from their natural beauty, rarity and value, they were believed by the magicians and occultists of bygone days to possess intrinsic virtues, which they could bestow upon those who wore them. This belief is implicit in the custom of each monarchy possessing its crown jewels or royal regalia and in the rings worn by bishops and other church dignitaries.

It appears also in the stories of many historic family heirlooms, especially among the old families of the more Celtic parts of the British Isles, namely Scotland, Wales and Ireland. Probably the most famous of such heirlooms is the Lee Penny, the heirloom of an ancient Scottish family, the Lockharts of Lee. This consists of a red stone mounted in the centre of a silver coin. It has long been believed to possess wonderful healing powers for the curing of diseased cattle; the method of its use being to immerse the talisman in water, and then give the water to the cattle to drink. Originally it was probably used for treating humans also.

The story attached to it says that it was brought home by one of the ancestors of the Lockharts of Lee who went to the Crusades and who received the stone as a ransom for a captured Saracen of high rank. However, the silver coin in which the red stone is mounted is an English groat of the reign of Edward IV; so its real origin is a mystery.

Among the English Crown Jewels is a wonderful stone of talismanic virtues, the Black Prince's ruby. It may be seen today mounted in the Imperial State Crown, among all the other splendours enshrined in the Jewel House at the Tower of London. The Black Prince was given the stone by his ally, Pedro the Cruel, who was said to have stolen it from the King of Granada, whom he murdered. In the following century, King Henry V took the stone and had it mounted in a coronet, which he wore upon his helmet at the Battle of Agincourt.

The story goes that this coronet saved his life, because in the course of the battle a blow aimed at the king's head was diverted by the coronet. Part of the coronet was broken off by the stroke; the very piece which contained the ruby. The story may be true or merely a romantic legend; but still today a mark may be seen upon the stone which might have been caused by the stroke of a sword.

The king was no doubt aware of the jewel's talismanic virtues and chose it for this reason. The ruby is a stone of

Mars, the planet which rules warfare and gives protection and victory in battle.

The astrological rulership of precious stones is an important factor in determining their virtues. Hence the idea of wearing one's birth-stone, in order to attract the best characteristics of the sign of the Zodiac under which one was born. Every sign of the Zodiac has its good and bad side, its strengths and its weaknesses. No sign is lucky or unlucky in itself.

However, the lists of birth-stones displayed in jewellers' windows are somewhat misleading, as they refer only to the month in which one was born, without mentioning the sign of the Zodiac. The changeover from one sign to another takes place around the 20th to the 22nd of each month. It varies a little each year, so that the precise time of the changeover can only be told by consulting an astrological ephemeris. (This is the name given to the yearly publications which supply detailed information of planetary movements, etc., for the use of astrologers).

Hence, a person born in March, for instance, may be under either Pisces or Aries, depending on which part of the month he or she was born in.

The list of birth-stones most generally agreed upon by jewellers is as follows:

January: Garnet.
February: Amethyst.
March: Bloodstone or Aquamarine.
April: Diamond.
May: Emerald.
June: Pearl or Moonstone.
July: Ruby.
August: Sardonyx or Peridot.
September: Sapphire.
October: Opal or Tourmaline.
November: Topaz.
December: Turqoise or Lapis Lazuli.

Few people realize the high antiquity from which such lists are derived. Their origin is to be found in the famous breast-plate of precious stones worn by the High Priest of Israel, as described in the Bible (*Exodus*, Chapter 28). This consisted of four rows of jewels, three to each row. Josephus, the great Jewish historian, who wrote his *Antiquities of the Jews* in the first century AD, tells us that the stones of the breastplate signified the twelve months of the year and the twelve signs of the Zodiac; while the two great sardonyx stones that were in the clasps on the High Priest's shoulders, symbolized the sun and the moon.

The Authorised Version of the Bible gives the stones of the breastplate as: a sardius, a topaz, and a carbuncle; an emerald, a sapphire, and a diamond; a ligure, an agate, and an amethyst; and a beryl, an onyx, and a jasper. Modern scholars, however, doubt the accuracy of this translation. They generally translate the list of stones as consisting of: carnelian, chrysolite and emerald; garnet, lapis lazuli and jasper (or possibly some form of corundum); jacinth, agate and amethyst; beryl, onyx and jade.

The custom of wearing birth-stones in modern times is thought to have originated in Poland, probably among the Jewish community there who traded in precious stones, and who were deeply interested in the mysticism of the sacred stones of the breastplate. It may have been spread throughout Europe by the fact that the Queen of France, wife of Louis XV, was the Polish Marie Leczinska; and the French court was the great centre of fashion and high society. So what the Queen of France wore and believed in was sure to be copied.

Here is an old Polish list of the birth-stones of the months, together with the particular virtue or blessing that each jewel was believed to bestow:

January: Garnet. Constancy.
February: Amethyst. Sincerity.
March: Bloodstone. Courage.
April: Diamond. Innocence.
May: Emerald. Success in love.
June: Agate. Health and long life.
July: Cornelian. Contentment.
August: Sardonyx. Happiness in marriage.
September: Chrysolite. Antidote to troubles of the mind.
October: Opal. Hope.
November: Topaz. Faithfulness.

December: Turquoise. Prosperity.

If we regard the bloodstone of March as being the obvious attribute of Aries (*circa* March 21st to April 21st), then we can interpret the rest of the stones accordingly, having found the starting-point of the Zodiac. Taurus takes the diamond, Gemini the emerald, Cancer the agate, Leo the cornelian, Virgo the sardonyx, Libra the chrysolite, Scorpio the opal, Sagittarius the topaz, Capricorn the turquoise, Aquarius the garnet and Pisces the amethyst.

The reason for associating the bloodstone with Aries is that it was a favourite talisman of soldiers and thus associated with Mars, the ruler of Aries. In addition to bestowing bravery upon its possessor, it was believed to have the power to staunch bleeding, when applied to wounds. The bloodstone is a smooth, opaque, greenish stone with little red specks in it, like spots of blood. Soldiers carried large bloodstones with them, which were smooth and rounded, of a suitable shape for binding on wounds. Their virtues were firmly believed in, and no doubt the coldness of the stone and the tight bandaging did help to stop bleeding, if the wound was not too severe.

Another stone particularly appropriate to Aries is the ruby, glowing red with the fire of Mars. Taurus (*circa* April 21st to May 21st) could compromise with the glittering or shining crystal, if diamonds are too costly; because crystal is ruled by the Moon, which is exalted in Taurus.

The emerald for Gemini is one of the most beautiful stones; but also, unfortunately, one of the most expensive. However, agates come in such great variety that they are often associated with versatile Mercury, the ruler of Gemini (*circa* May 21st to June 21st). I would definitely prefer the pearl or the moonstone to the agate as the mascot of Cancer (*circa* June 21st to July 21st), because this sign is ruled by the Moon. A strange thing about some agates is the way in which they display amazingly natural pictures in the stone, when it is cut and polished. I myself have seen a large nodule of agate which contained a startling likeness of a human eye — a natural amulet if ever there was one. This faculty of depicting things is an attribute of Mercury.

Warm, red cornelian certainly suits Leo (*circa* July 21st to

August 21st); but so, I think, does amber, with its beautiful shades of red and gold. Leo is ruled by the Sun. The sardonyx for Virgo (*circa* August 21st to September 21st) is another stone which comes in variegated form, associating it with Mercury, the ruler of Virgo. It displays bands of white and red, which were often cleverly carved into cameos in times past; the white part being used for the figures while the red formed the background.

The chrysolite for Libra (*circa* September 21st to October 21st) literally means 'the golden stone'; but its colour actually varies from golden-yellow to olive-green. Perhaps the most beautiful variety of it is the light green stone called the peridot. The belief in its virtues as an antidote to troubles of the mind goes back to Roman times. The Romans wore peridots set in gold to protect them against melancholy and against illusions and fears, especially those caused by enchantment.

The opal is often regarded as being a rather sinister stone and it is certainly a very costly one. Hence people born under Scorpio (*circa* October 21st to November 21st) might care to take the alternative of aquamarine. The name of this stone means 'sea water', and Scorpio is the fixed sign of water. Another alternative is serpentine, literally 'snakelike stone', from its fancied resemblance to the markings of a snake; the serpent being one of the symbols of Scorpio.

The lovely topaz for Sagittarius, with all its warm shades of brownish-gold, could hardly fail to please. Nor is it excessively rare and costly. There is a variety of it found in Scotland and known as the cairngorm. However, if Jupiter ruling the natives of Sagittarius (*circa* November 21st to December 21st) makes them desire a richer talisman, then the heavenly blue of the sapphire certainly seems appropriate; because in mythology the god Jupiter or Zeus was ruler of the skies.

The turquoise for Capricorn (*circa* December 21st to January 21st) is a stone almost universally esteemed as an amulet. It is particularly valued by the Tibetans, who use it a great deal in jewellery. The Red Indians of North America know it also, and regard it as being a stone of magical virtues. It is one of those jewels of which legend says that it becomes pale when its owner is in danger, thus serving as a warning that some peril is at hand.

Other Capricornian stones are jet and black onyx. Real jet has similar electrical properties to amber; hence its old name of 'black amber'. It is one of the oldest of magical stones; necklaces of polished jet have been found in prehistoric graves. However, the buyer should beware, because much that is sold as jet is really only black glass. One of the homes of real jet is Whitby, in Yorkshire, where attractive jewellery of jet is still obtainable.

As for the mysterious black onyx, this is a stone which seems to have stolen something of midnight itself and enclosed it in its shining surface. In ancient days, a concave piece of highly polished black onyx was used as a magic mirror, more potent even than a crystal ball to induce clairvoyance. The famous 'show-stone' of the Elizabethan magician, Dr Dee, was a mirror of this type; though accounts differ as to just what mineral it was made of. Sometimes the black onyx displays bands of white and it can then be skilfully cut and polished to resemble an eye — another potent amulet against the peril of the evil eye, which was so much dreaded by people of olden times.

The stone given for Aquarius (*circa* January 21st to February 21st), the garnet, is both beautiful and reasonably within the means of most people. However, it is rather hard to see its relevance to the airy sign of Aquarius, ruled by Saturn and Uranus; though the garnet's fiery red glow, like a burning ember, is welcome in the coldest days of winter, which occur in the time of year that Aquarius rules. My own feeling is that the garnet is more suitable for Capricorn, the sign in which fiery Mars is exalted.

Other possible Aquarian stones are the whitish-blue chalcedony, with its resemblance to a lightly-clouded blue sky, and the blue zircon, which shows the bright electric blue of Uranus. However, perhaps the most 'heavenly' stone of all appropriate to Aquarius, the fixed sign of air, is the star sapphire, which displays in its polished blue depths the perfect image of a star, surrounded by shining rays of light, which cross inside the stone to produce the 'star'. These are believed in the East to represent the powers of Faith, Hope and Destiny. Hence the star sapphire is one of the most wonderful and potent of talismanic stones, attracting good fortune and warding off evil.

The amethyst for Pisces (*circa* February 21st to March 21st) is one of the stones ruled by Jupiter, the planet that rules Pisces, and hence it is fully appropriate, its rich purple and violet hues according well with the rather mystical tendencies of the sign of Pisces. It is a favourite stone for the rings worn by bishops and other highly-placed ecclesiastics. It has a calming and soothing influence and a time-honoured legend says of it that it preserves its wearer from drunkenness and excessive passions.

Another precious substance appropriate to Pisces is coral; because the co-ruler of Pisces is Neptune, and it is a watery sign. Iridescent shell, of which modern jewellery is sometimes made, would be harmonious with Pisces also.

Some other beautiful and reasonably priced gem-stones are the apple-green chrysoprase, the rose quartz, and the tawny golden-striped crocidolite. The delicate green of chrysoprase is the green of growing things, of new life. I feel that it would be appropriate to Virgo, with its suggestion of youth and virginity. Rose quartz is suggestive of Venus; it is the colour of sentiment and romance, and hence would be appropriate to Libra, the sign ruled by Venus. (Taurus is also ruled by Venus; but rose quartz seems to me more in harmony with airy Libra than earthy Taurus). The golden gleams of crocidolite make it a natural choice for natives of the Sun's own sign, Leo.

The lore of precious stones is an inexhaustible subject; but I hope that enough has been said here to enable readers to make a choice of a talismanic gem-stone which will be both suitable to the time of their nativity, and within their price-range. Those who wish to study further will find much helpful and fascinating information in the following books:

The Curious Lore of Precious Stones, by George Frederick Kunz (first published 1913, reprinted by Dover Publications, Inc., New York, 1971).

Amulets and Talismans, by Sir E. A. Wallis Budge (first published 1930, reprinted by Collier Books, New York, 1970).

The Book of Talismans, Amulets and Zodiacal Gems, by William Thomas and Kate Pavitt (Riders, London, 1922 and recently reprinted).

Apart from precious stones and their virtues, there are other time-honoured amulets and talismans, consisting of things in some form or design which is believed to be magical. For instance, we see jewellery produced in the shape of the ankh cross, the swastika, the scarab, the Hand of Fatima, the horseshoe, the four-leaved clover, the two interlaced triangles which form the Star of David and so on. All these are loosely described as 'lucky charms'; but what is their real meaning?

Some of them, like the ankh cross and the scarab, go back to ancient Egypt. Others, like the swastika, may be even older. It is a great pity that the swastika has become unpopular, as a result of its adoption by the followers of Adolf Hitler; because it is one of the most venerable and world-wide symbols. Its distribution on both sides of the Atlantic has caused some occultists to believe that it originated in the lost continent of Atlantis.

The swastika is known to the American Indians, who regard it as a sacred and magical sign. It also appears among the remains of prehistoric Mexico, notably upon many of the famous stone tablets discovered by William Niven and described by Colonel James Churchward in his books about that other sunken continent, Mu or Lemuria. Indeed, to record all the various manifestations of this mysterious symbol would need a chapter to itself. It can be found upon the thrones of Tibetan lamas of high rank and upon very old church bells in English belfries. The people of ancient China revered it, and so did the people of Troy. Its name, *swastika*, comes from Sanskrit, the sacred language of India, and means happiness, well-being, good luck.

Some particularly interesting forms of the swastika are those which appear upon the mysterious stone monuments of prehistoric Scotland. These are generally attributed to the Picts. A notable example is the Newton Stone, found in Aberdeenshire, which displays a swastika surrounded by an inscription in an unknown alphabet.

One of the most famous talismans of the ancient East was the signet ring of Jenghis Khan, a large gold ring set with a magnificent ruby, upon which was engraved the sign of the swastika. It was preserved with the greatest care and secrecy among the Buddhist lamas of Mongolia, as its possession was believed to confer great power and protection.

That great nineteenth-century occultist, Madame Blavatsky, explains the swastika as being basically an equal-armed cross, a symbol far older than Christianity. The upright line represents the masculine influence, the horizontal line the feminine one. From the union of two opposites, masculine and feminine, positive and negative, comes all manifestation. Then lines are added to the cross, signifying motion, the Wheel of Life, or cyclic law. Thus the swastika appears, with its four arms symbolizing birth, life, death, and immortality. There are also the four winds, the four seasons and the four elements; and all these are summed up in the swastika.

Much argument has taken place over the question of which way the arms of the swastika should point, to the right or to the left. Some say the former is most beneficent and fortunate and some say the latter. Both forms are found in ancient art, and apparently regarded as being equally sacred. Hitler favoured the swastika with arms pointing to the right; but the swastika adopted by Madame Blavatsky as part of the emblem of the Theosophical Society points in the other direction.

The ankh cross is the ancient Egyptian symbol of life and immortality. The gods and goddesses of Egypt are generally depicted holding this emblem in their hands, grasping it by the loop as if it were a key; hence it is sometimes called 'The Key of Life'. It occurs in hieroglyphic inscriptions as the symbol meaning 'life'; for instance, in the royal cartouche of the Pharaoh Tutankh-amun, whose name has been translated by Egyptologists as meaning 'The Living Image of Amen'.

Like the swastika, the ankh cross dates back to unknown antiquity. Some authorities have believed it to be a conventionalized figure of a sandal-strap, symbolizing the power to go, to travel onwards; and conveying the idea of the human soul as the pilgrim of eternity. However, it seems perhaps more likely that the ankh cross represents the union of male and female, the creative powers of life. The looped part of the ankh, by its oval shape, signifies the opening of the vagina; while the T-shaped part is a simplified figure of the penis and testicles.

There are many ancient amulets which were quite openly

The Magician evoking a spirit. Note seal of Solomon design on front of altar

made in the shape of the human genital organs. They were life symbols and hence luck symbols. However, the highly evolved and delicate art of ancient Egypt portrayed the ankh cross as an artistic, hieroglyphic form of a primordial idea.

The scarab is another ancient Egyptian amulet of tremendous antiquity. It represents the god Kephra, the sun at night, hidden below the horizon yet potent to come forth and bring the dawn. He was represented as a beetle, because of the habits of this insect, which the Egyptians regarded as sacred. Beetles have beautiful, iridescent wing-cases which reflect the light like jewels; they fly about at dusk, when the sun is sinking, and most important of all, this particular beetle, the scarab, lays its eggs in the dung of animals, which it then rolls into a ball bigger than itself.

The Egyptians saw the little insect propelling this ball with its hind legs; and they compared it to the mysterious power which propelled the sun on its apparent course. They saw the ball eventually pushed into a hole in the ground, even as the sun disappeared beneath the western horizon. Then, one day, the eggs would hatch within their warm cover and new life burst forth; even as the sun was reborn each morning.

Hence the scarab became a potent symbol of resurrection, of eternal life; and, naturally, it is frequently found interred with Egyptian mummies. But it was also a popular amulet for the living. The flat underside of the scarab was often engraved with words of magical power, or with the name of a Pharaoh.

The amulet might be made from some semi-precious stone, such as cornelian; or it might be of stone or pottery, coloured with a blue or green glaze. Like many Egyptian amulets, it would often have a hole pierced through it, so that it could be conveniently hung round the neck or set in a ring.

Throughout Moslem countries today, and for many centuries past, a popular amulet is the conventionalized figure of a hand. It may be seen hung upon the wall of a living-room; or a smaller version is worn round the neck. These amulets are often beautifully made of gold or silver-gilt filigree work, and set with precious stones. They are called the Hand of Fatima, out of respect for Fatima, the daughter of Mohammed. Actually, however, the hand as an amulet is even older than the days when Mohammed was founding the religion of Islam.

It derives from the natural gesture of raising the hand to ward off evil, especially the peril of the evil eye. Such protective hands are often set with bright blue turquoises, for this reason. The colour blue, the clear hue of heaven, is believed throughout the East to have the power of averting evil occult influence, as already noted in Chapter V.

A familiar talismanic figure is the two interlaced triangles which form the Star of David, the symbol of the Jewish religion. This six-pointed star, formed by the two triangles, is also called the Seal of Solomon. The Biblical King Solomon was believed in the ancient world to have been a great magician, able to command powerful genii and even demons and force them to do his bidding. Two of the most famous grimoires, or books of ceremonial magic, are called *The Key of Solomon the King*, and *The Goetia, or Lesser Key of Solomon.* Whether in fact either book really had anything to do with King Solomon is highly problematical. However, the basic form of the six-pointed star occurs over and over again in ancient books of magic; and always as a powerful amulet to protect the magician against evil forces.

It is probably even older than the time of King Solomon, because it is also found in the age-old magical lore of India. The Indian form of it shows the symbol of the sun in the centre of the interlaced triangles. The modern Jewish version sometimes displays in the centre the Hebrew letters of the word *Mazeltov*, meaning 'good luck'.

The upward-pointing triangle is the elemental symbol of fire, the downward-pointing one that of water. Fire is regarded as a masculine element and water as a feminine one. So we have again the idea of the union of masculine and feminine, displayed this time in the form of interlaced triangles. Also, when the symbol of the sun is drawn in the centre of the figure, we have the implied presence of the six other visible heavenly bodies of greatest significance, distributed around the points of the star; namely, Saturn, Jupiter, Mars, Venus, Mercury and the Moon. These together with the Sun make up the sacred seven whose influence is so important in all ancient magic.

Another important magical sigil is the five-pointed star, called the Pentagram or Pentacle. This, too, may be found as

The Upright Pentagram, the Blazing Star of White Magic,
drawn in the form of the Endless Knot

a piece of magical jewellery; though perhaps not so frequently as the Seal of Solomon. In mediaeval times, it acquired the curious name of the Goblins' Cross; and it was also called the Endless Knot, because it can be drawn in one continuous line, without lifting the pen from the paper. Like the Seal of Solomon, it was believed to be a potent amulet against evil; but for this purpose it had to be drawn with one point upwards. It then represented the power of the spirit ruling over the four elements of the material world.

The Pentagram was drawn in this way, or a representation of it hung, at the doors and windows of houses, to keep out evil spirits. In the old folk-song, "Green Grow the Rushes, O!", occurs the line, "Five is the symbol at your door" — referring to this time-honoured use of the magical Pentagram.

Leaves of the lucky four-leaved clover are sometimes worn enclosed in a locket, or a representation of the leaf in gold or silver may be seen. How this little plant acquired such a magical reputation is not exactly known; but the old folk rhyme about it runs as follows:

> One leaf for fame,
> And one for wealth,
> And one for a faithful lover,
> And one to bring you glorious health,
> Are all in a four-leaved clover.

The lucky horseshoe is really a form of the crescent, which derives its fortunate influence from the moon goddess. Whether called Isis, Diana, Artemis, Tanith, Ishtar, Astarte, Hecate, Cerridwen, or any of the myriad of names by which she was known, the moon goddess was the ancient mistress of magic and enchantment. The figures of the lunar crescent and the horse appear together on ancient British coins, notably those minted by the Iceni, the people of Queen Boadicea.

The horseshoe also carries with it the magic of the smith and his craft. All good blacksmiths were supposed to be natural magicians. Our Anglo-Saxon ancestors delighted in the tales of Wayland the Smith and his magical powers. In later years, with the spread of Christianity, legends were told of doughty St Dunstan, who worked as a blacksmith and had frequent magical contests with the Devil. Cold iron, especially in the form of a horseshoe, was a protection against the mischief of the fairies and all sorts of uncanny beings.

The luckiest horseshoe is that which you find yourself, by accident, cast upon the road. You should nail it up over your door, for luck; but be sure to have the ends of the horseshoe pointing upwards, or the luck will run out. Only the blacksmith himself is privileged to hang a lucky horseshoe with the ends down, to pour out the luck upon the forge.

A potent natural amulet and talisman for good fortune, is a piece of lodestone. This is iron ore containing natural magnetic properties, hence it is sometimes called magnetite. Though not as strong as a manufactured magnet, it will nevertheless pick up steel pins and needles. In appearance, it is a mere rough, blueish-grey stone with metallic veins in it; yet an old rhyme pays tribute to its magical virtues:

> The lodestone is the stone, the only stone alone,
> Deserving praise above the rest, whose virtues are unknown.
> The diamond bright, the sapphire brave, are stones that bear the name;
> But flatter not, and tell the truth, lodestone deserves the same.

To carry a lodestone was believed to bestow health, vigour and sexual attractiveness. It strengthened magical powers and dispelled evil spirits. Wealthy magicians wore their lodestone in a little cage of gold or silver filigree, hung from a chain around the neck. The less wealthy carried it in a small bag of soft leather, together with some magical herbs. This might be hung from a string round the neck, or worn somehow close to the skin. Sometimes the bag contained a pair of small, twin lodestones, cleaving together by their own magnetic power. This was considered to be a very potent charm to attract love.

One often sees rings, bracelets and necklaces fashioned in the form of a snake, or of two serpents intertwined. This is another form of jewellery that was originally magical, though today often worn merely for ornament. The sacred serpent appears upon the crowns of Egyptian Pharaohs and in the temple carvings of ancient India. Hermes, the herald of the gods of Greece and patron of magic, is portrayed carrying the caduceus, a wand with two serpents twined about it.

In the latter case, the twin serpents represent the two interacting forces, positive and negative, which manifest throughout nature — a basic idea which we have seen frequently repeated in different forms.

The snake is also a symbol of spiritual power. To the people of olden time, it seemed a mysterious creature, because of the way in which it glided without legs. Anyone who watches a serpent travelling over the ground with amazing speed, must feel something of this strangeness. Moreover, the serpent renews itself by shedding its complete skin and this habit has caused it to become the emblem of rebirth and immortality.

It is widely believed that snakes can hypnotize birds and small animals, so that they become entranced and allow the snake to swallow them. Thus the snake has come to represent mysterious occult power and as such, it is frequently depicted upon the paraphernalia of magic. Sometimes the serpent is shown holding its tail in its mouth. The Greeks called this figure of the encircled serpent the *Ouroborous* and regarded it as a symbol of infinity and eternity.

VII
Magic of Sex

For nearly two thousand years, in the western world at any rate, the idea of sex has been almost synonymous with that of sin. This unhappy aberration in man's philosophy, productive of so much misery and frustration, has been in complete contrast with earlier ways of thinking among the pagans of the ancient world and with a good deal of eastern mystical philosophy also.

Upon some of the ancient temples of India, magnificent sculptures portray gods and goddesses in every conceivable variety of sexual embrace. In old-time Tibet also, the deities were depicted in this manner. The sacred *Yab-Yum*, or 'Father-Mother' pictures, showed male divinities united in sexual climax with their female counterparts.

The basis for this conjunction of sex and spirituality is the world-wide observation of the interplay of opposites throughout manifested nature. The followers of so chaste and ascetic a philosopher as Pythagoras bore witness to this idea in ancient Greece. To the mediaeval alchemists, the Great Work came from the union of opposites. The Chinese sages based both philosophy and magic upon the interplay of the complementary forces which they called *Yang* and *Yin*.

Yang and *Yin* were the fundamentals of the universe. *Yang* was positive, *Yin* was negative. *Yang* represented masculinity, the Sun, the heavens, the day; while *Yin* ruled femininity, the Moon, the earth, the night. The *Tao*, or absolute divinity, was depicted by a sacred diagram showing the *Yang* and *Yin* forces locked within a circle.

The sacred four-lettered name of God, the Tetragrammaton, which the translators of the Bible have rendered, somewhat misleadingly, as 'Jehovah', also contains this idea. It is composed of four Hebrew letters, *Yod, He, Vau* and *He* again. The mystical Rabbis who formulated the Hebrew Qabalah or Kabbalah (a word meaning secret tradition handed down), said that the *Yod* of Tetragrammaton means the Divine Masculinity, the first *He* means the Divine Femininity, the *Vau* means their supernal union and the final *He* means the material universe which results from it.

The word 'Jehovah' is in fact similar to a number of other divine names, or appellations of the Supreme Deity, which occur in those Graeco-Egyptian systems of magic that have come to be known as Gnostic. Such, for instance, is the word IAOOUEI, which magicians of Alexandria in Egypt used as a divine name and a word of power. It has been conjectured that this word is derived from the sounds made by people at the moment of sexual climax. Very similar is IO EVOHE the ecstatic cry of the dancers in the Greek Mysteries; and this, too, could have had its origin in the involuntary sounds of orgasm.

The mystic word IO is composed of letters in the shape of an upright and a circle; symbols which represent the male and female organs of generation. The same idea in prehistoric Britain was expressed in stone. Some of the mighty stones of Avebury, of unknown antiquity, are composed alternately of tall uprights, representing the male principle, or *phallus*, and broader, diamond-shaped stones, representing the female genital orifice, or *cteis*. Two of the biggest of these stones are known locally as Adam and Eve.

This time-honoured concept is even more plainly expressed by a group of prehistoric stones near Penzance in Cornwall, known in the old Cornish language as the *Men-an-Tol*. This group consists of two upright stones, with a broader stone between them. This broad, central stone has a large hole painstakingly carved through its centre, making it a feminine symbol. These stones have been revered from time immemorial as possessing magical powers. Sickly children were believed to be made stronger by being helped to crawl through the holed stone of the *Men-an-Tol*. This is probably a folk-memory of an ancient rite of rebirth.

Another group of prehistoric stones in Britain, with a long history of folklore and magic, are the Rollright Stones, near

The Maypole as it used to be in old-time London.
Note upright-and-circle symbolism

Long Compton, on the border between Oxfordshire and Warwickshire. These consist of a circle of large stones, originally more conspicuous than they are now as many have sunk into the earth. Outside this circle is a massive upright stone called the King Stone. The circle of stones is about one hundred feet in diameter, and the King Stone is nearly nine feet tall.

This wonderful group of stones now has a modern road running through it, between the King Stone and the circle; but its ancient magic is still potent. The spirit of its basic design is evidently sexual; the upright and the circle, the masculine and the feminine. One legend about the Rollright Stones says that if a childless woman desired to be cured of her barrenness, she should go to the Rollright Stones secretly, on the night of the full moon, strip off her clothes and dance three times naked around the circle and then go up to the King Stone and embrace it, standing so that its shadow cast by the moonlight covers her.

No doubt this ritual was surreptitiously done by many Cotswold country wives in days long ago. Today, a would-be practitioner of the ritual would need to beware of passing cars on the road (though it is fairly lonely one) and she would also need sandals to protect her feet from the debris left behind by picnickers.

Ritual nudity as a magical practice is very old. The naked dances organized by the pagan cult of witchcraft in times past were denounced by the Church; but they still took place. In those days, when the countryside was much more thinly populated than it is today, large bonfires could be lit in lonely places, to provide light and warmth, and a gay, glowing centre of magic flame to dance around. By dancing naked, in a state of mind of 'oneness with nature', witches contacted the universal life energy, and felt themselves revitalized. Even in modern days, the ashes of bonfires have been found at the Rollright Stones — fires believed locally to have been lit for purposes of witchcraft.

The ancient rites of fertility and vitality belonging to the Old Religion of Nature, still take place secretly in the countryside of Britain, as they do elsewhere in Europe and America, particularly at the full moon. They are done for luck, for enjoyment and for the continuance of age-old tradition.

One such ritual involves a man and a woman dancing seven times round a large tree, preferably an oak. Both have to be naked, so a warm summer night of the full moon is preferred. She pretends to be trying to escape and he to pursue her. But at the seventh round of the dance, she allows him to catch her and they have intercourse beneath the tree. At the end of the rite, a leaf is plucked from the tree and moistened with the sexual fluids that have been mingled in the woman's vagina. This leaf is considered to be a powerful talisman and may be carried to bring good fortune, or used in other magical ways.

A similar rite is performed around a bonfire, lit within an old stone circle; and this may have been the purpose of the bonfires of which traces were found at the Rollright Stones, as mentioned above. This is seldom done today, as it is too likely to be seen and to attract the attention of outsiders. When it is performed, however, the woman carries a small branch with green leaves on it, as she dances. A leaf is plucked from the branch and used as above, and the rest of the branch is burned on the fire.

When the rite is finished, the fire, which need only be a small one, is extinguished by pouring upon it a libation of wine or cider. This is taken to the ceremony in a special flask or bottle marked with witchcraft signs, as nothing common should be brought into the magic circle. Each of the participants takes a drink from the bottle, and they repeat an old form of words:

As merry we have met,
As merry we have been,
So merry may we part,
And merry meet again.

Then the rest of the wine or cider is poured upon the fire.

If no ancient stone circle is available, the witches may use thirteen ordinary stones to mark out a circle to work in. These stones are usually removed afterwards, so that no tell-tale traces remain and the ashes of the fire are ascribed to picnickers or gypsies.

The Christian church proclaimed sexual intercourse to have been ordained for one purpose only, namely the procreation of

The dance of the witches' Sabbat

children; to use it and especially to enjoy it for any other purpose was sin. But the secret practitioners of magic have always denied this idea. Sex, they say, has three functions: propagation of the race, sheer enjoyment, and revitalization by the exchange of vital magnetism. For the last function, actual intercourse was not absolutely necessary. It could take place between man and woman by touching, kissing and embracing, especially if both partners were nude. The only proviso was that they must be in sympathy with each other, so that their auras blended harmoniously.

Modern medical science supports these contentions, insofar as it has proved that a woman can only conceive for a brief time of a few days out of her monthly cycle of ovulation and menstruation. Yet she is fully capable of enjoying sexual intercourse throughout the cycle, except when she is actually menstruating. So what are the rest of the days of the cycle for?

As there are three functions of sex, so it exists in three forms of activity: auto-sexual, homosexual and heterosexual. That is, sexual enjoyment by oneself, or with a member of one's own sex, or with a member of the opposite sex. Again, the idea of the magical number three, or the triad, appears. All these forms of sexual activity have been used, both in magic and religion, from time immemorial.

Old-time moralists made a tremendous fuss about so-called 'self-abuse', or masturbation. It was even supposed to be 'the sin against the Holy Ghost' as well as being responsible for just about everything from criminal lunacy to ingrowing toenails. Today, however, psychologists regard it as a perfectly natural thing; so what was the agitation really about? Just possibly, because of the use of human sexual secretions for magical purposes. This applies both to the male sperm and to the secretion of the Bartholin glands in the female. The latter are a pair of small glands, situated one on either side of the entrance to the vagina, that secrete a fluid which moistens the vagina when the female is sexually aroused.

These human sexual secretions, both male and female, are alluded to under the symbolism of alchemy; the male as the blood or essence of the Red Lion, and the female as the gluten or essence of the White Eagle. The 'Lion' is the emblem of

Leo, the fixed sign of fire; the 'Eagle' is the emblem of the higher aspect of Scorpio, the fixed sign of water. Fire is regarded as a masculine element and water as a feminine one. Similarly, the alchemical vessels could represent the sexual organs. The athanor could be a synonym for the penis and the cucurbit (a gourd-shaped vessel) for the vagina. Old alchemical manuscripts sometimes have illustrations of these vessels, in which their shapes are clearly reminiscent of sexual significance. The mingled sexual fluids constitute the 'First Matter', out of which is transmuted the 'Elixir of Life'.

The strange symbolism of alchemy was one way in which secret brotherhoods concealed the sexual nature of their rites, which might otherwise have been denounced as 'abominations' simply because they involved sex. (Although, of course, not all alchemical symbolism should be interpreted in this way).

Aleister Crowley, in his notorious book *Magick in Theory and Practice*, had a joke at the expense of the credulous, when he wrote that "a male child of perfect innocence and high intelligence" was the most suitable victim for a magical sacrifice; claiming that he himself had been making such a sacrifice "on an average about 150 times every year" for several years past! What Crowley actually meant was that he used his own semen for magical purposes, but even some present-day writers have swallowed the bait and shudderingly declared that Crowley and his followers were criminals who performed human sacrifices. (*Magick in Theory and Practise* was first privately printed in Paris in 1929. It has since been reprinted by Castle Books of New York.)

The idea behind this practice is that the vital essences of the body give off power, which can be directed by the mind and will of the magician for some specific end. In the case of animal sacrifice, it is the freshly-spilt blood which gives off this vital power. But, say those magicians who practise sexual rites, why use such a crude, brutal and cruel method as killing some living creature, when there are much pleasanter means at hand?

Magica sexualis, or sexual magic, has been the well-kept secret of the inner circles of many occult brotherhoods, of both east and west. It has been disguised in curious symbolism and

A group of Etruscan dieties from a mirror back depicting
the carefree rites of ancient times

abstruse terms, because hitherto frank discussion of such ideas has not been possible. Because sexual enjoyment was the great sin, any ritual which involved sex must automatically be black magic and devil-worship. Quite a good deal of this mentality still lingers, even in our own day.

The pagans of ancient times thought differently. They believed that which gave pleasure to humans also gave pleasure to the gods; in other words, the gods were happy to see man happy. This idea was handed down in the Orient for many centuries. M. C. Poinsot, in *L'Amour et la Magie* (Paris, 1926), quotes from a French translation of a famous Arabic treatise on sexual matters, written by Kohdja Omer Aleby Aben Othman: *"La copulation est le plus grand et le plus saint des cantiques"*, "Copulation is the greatest and holiest song of praise".

Farther east, the Tantriks of India, those mystics who follow the old traditions called *Tantras*, perform a kind of five-fold sacrament of union with nature. Like the magicians of the west, they recognize five elements, the fifth being spirit or *akasha*. Their communion is called the *Panchamakara*, or 'Five Ms', because it involves five things beginning with the letter M:

Wine (*madya*) for the element of fire.
Meat (*mangsa*) for air.
Fish (*matsya*) for water.
Bread (*mudra*) for earth.
Sexual intercourse (*maithuna*) for spirit.

The priestess with whom the sexual act takes place within the consecrated circle, is regarded as the living personification of Shakti, the goddess of universal nature.

They find the sacred elements of life present symbolically within the sexual act itself. The hardness felt as the penis penetrates the vagina, represents earth. The flow of semen and moisture represents water. The rubbing together of the genitals is like the rubbing of sticks to produce fire. The movement of the two bodies is like the movement of air. The passion of the climax produces pleasure and the nature of pleasure or ecstasy is *akasha*.

The penis is symbolically referred to as the *vajra* or 'thunderbolt', and the vagina as the lotus-flower. Hence one meaning of the mystic *mantram*, or sacred phrase: *Aum mani padme hum*, "Hail to the jewel in the lotus".

Another Tantrik belief is that at the moment of sexual orgasm a quantity of vital magnetism is released. If this occurs simultaneously with both partners in coition, then there is an harmonious exchange of vitality which is beneficial to both. Hence the kind of sexual intercourse all too common in western countries, where the only thing that matters to the man is his own satisfaction, would be quite useless from this point of view.

Two things are evidently very important for the purpose of sexual magic; namely, that the partners should be in complete harmony with each other, and that they should be sexually potent. Occultism has a good deal of advice to give upon both these points.

By comparing the horoscopes of two people, a skilled astrologer can tell if they are likely to be suited to each other or not. This requires correct horoscopes to be cast for both; but a rough rule-of-thumb guide is that people born under birth signs of the same element, earth, fire, air or water, are likely to get on well together, because such signs will be in trine aspect to each other on the map of the Zodiac, and this is the most favourable and harmonious aspect.

The fire signs are Aries, Leo and Sagittarius. The water signs are Cancer, Scorpio and Pisces. The air signs are Libra, Aquarius and Gemini. The earth signs are Capricorn, Taurus and Virgo.

A phenomenon I have often noticed with regard to people's birth signs, is that people born under signs which are opposite to one another in the Zodiac are often violently attracted to each other, but the attraction does not last. It is more in the nature of infatuation than genuine love. This seems to bear out the old saying that opposites attract. Such attraction may be great fun while it lasts; but the end is usually stormy.

Such Zodiacal opposites are Aries and Libra, Taurus and Scorpio, Gemini and Sagittarius, Cancer and Capricorn, Leo and Aquarius, Virgo and Pisces.

People who are definitely unlikely to be in harmony with each other, are those whose birth signs are what the astrologers call in square aspect to each other, because this is a difficult and inharmonious aspect.

Aries is square to Cancer and Capricorn.
Taurus is square to Leo and Aquarius.
Gemini is square to Virgo and Pisces.
Cancer is square to Libra and Aries.
Leo is square to Scorpio and Taurus.
Virgo is square to Sagittarius and Gemini.
Libra is square to Cancer and Capricorn.
Scorpio is square to Leo and Aquarius.
Sagittarius is square to Pisces and Virgo.
Capricorn is square to Libra and Aries.
Aquarius is square to Scorpio and Taurus.
Pisces is square to Sagittarius and Gemini.

In addition to this astrological guidance, some occultists believe that there will be more excitement and satisfaction in a love affair if a fair person mates with a dark one and vice versa. Blondes, they say, are 'electric' and brunettes 'magnetic'. Such expressions, of course, are figurative; but they are an attempt to express the difference between the auras of fair people and dark people, when it comes to a question of how their particular vibrations will blend.

The ways in which people have sought for occult means of securing sexual potency are so numerous, that the study of them forms a branch of *magica sexualis* in itself. People have been willing to swallow the most revolting concoctions, if only this end could be achieved thereby. Yet medical science assures us that, in most cases, the effect of such 'love potions' could only be psychological.

Nevertheless, when it comes to such an intimate thing as one's sexual relationships, psychology can be a very powerful influence. Many a supposedly impotent man has been made so by a nagging wife, for instance; there has been nothing physically wrong with him. Likewise, many allegedly frigid women have really been simply unable to respond to a selfish, clumsy and sexually ignorant man.

Leaving aside the horrid and often poisonous recipes recommended in old books of magic as aphrodisiacs, and the rich and expensive foods such as truffles and oysters, widely believed to have the same effect, is there anything left which is a genuine aphrodisiac or stimulant of sexual potency?

In the way of an actual potion, that is, something to be

drunk, the only proven aphrodisiac is alcohol — *in small but powerful quantities*. Therefore, it would seem that the ideal love potion to be taken by two people before they start to embrace, is a good liqueur. Many liqueurs, in fact, have a secret reputation as aphrodisiacs. Creme de Menthe is notable in this respect; oil of peppermint, which it contains, has been considered an aphrodisiac since the days of ancient Greece. Another liqueur has the significant title of Parfait Amour, 'Perfect Love'.

However, the most bewitching of liqueurs is undoubtedly Strega. The word *strega* is Italian for 'witch'; and the story goes that this liqueur was originally made as a witches' potion. It comes from the district of Benevento, in Italy, well-known for its legends of witchcraft, and reputed to be a time-honoured centre of *La Vecchia Religione*, 'the Old Religion'. The witches' potion is now made commercially; but a memento of its origin may be seen upon the bottle, which bears a lively little picture of a witches' dance.

Drambuie is another stimulating drink, reputed to have been a favourite with Bonnie Prince Charlie, the Young Pretender, when he was adventuring in Scotland. Advocaat is a stimulant and restorative, containing egg-yolks. Kummel is a liqueur flavoured with the aromatic seeds of cumin and caraway, which have a tonic effect. Nor are the virtues of Chartreuse and Benedictine to be overlooked, in spite of the fact that these liqueurs are traditionally made by monks.

Remember, however, that *all* liqueurs are meant to be taken in small quantities only, to be savoured and sipped delicately from beautiful liqueur glasses. Haste and excess will defeat their own ends; instead of being stimulated, all you will get is a sick headache.

Good wine also tends to have an aphrodisiac effect; but beer or spirits are less suitable. Mead, that most time-honoured of drinks, has an excellent reputation for building sexual potency. It is not generally realized that our term 'honeymoon' takes its name from this fact. Among our Celtic and Anglo-Saxon ancestors, newly-wedded couples used to drink plenty of mead for a month after their wedding, to make them strong and fertile. Mead is made from honey, hence this was the 'honeymoon'. When we remember how health food specialists today praise the virtues of honey, there may well be sound sense in this old belief. Once again, however, moderation is advised — really good old-fashioned mead, which can still be found in the English countryside, is powerful stuff.

A powerful stimulant to the senses is the right sort of perfume. Two perfumes which have the reputation of being aphrodisiacs are musk and patchouli. The latter first came to the western world when it was used to scent the luxurious Indian shawls which were so popular with Victorian ladies; and it soon became the favourite scent of high-class women of pleasure. Consequently, it tended to be frowned upon in respectable society, and a certain air of moral disapproval still seems to cling to it. The aphrodisiac properties of musk have been known throughout the East for many centuries. These and other oriental scents can be obtained in the form of cones and joss-sticks, to burn as incense. Indeed, I have seen packets of joss-sticks of the perfume known as *Javaji*, unashamedly labelled "No. 1 Bedroom Special".

Other sexually exciting scents are *Ylang-Ylang* and jasmine. The former name means 'flower of flowers'; it is obtained from richly scented flowers which grow in Madagascar. The Chinese of olden times called the jasmine 'sweetness in women' and it was a favourite with oriental concubines.

Perhaps the strangest of all aphrodisiacs and yet one which has been proven to work, is mild flagellation upon the buttocks. The operative word, however, is *mild*. I am not dealing here with the practices of sadism or masochism; but simply with the use of flagellation as a stimulant, which it undoubtedly is. Indeed, it may surprise many people to learn that a number of highly-respected physicians of bygone days recommended the use of whipping or birching for this purpose, provided it was not applied with too heavy a hand.

This fact is commented on by an erudite Victorian writer, John Davenport, in a curious book called *Aphrodisiacs and Anti-Aphrodisiacs; Three Essays on the Powers of Reproduction*; first published, privately printed, in London in 1869. He says:

> As an erotic stimulant, more particularly, it may be observed that, considering the many intimate and sympathetic relations existing between the nervous branches of the extremity of the spinal marrow, it is impossible to doubt that flagellation exercised upon the buttocks and the adjacent parts has a powerful effect upon the organs of generation.

(Davenport's very interesting book has been reissued in our own day under the title of *Aphrodisiacs and Love Stimulants*, edited by Alan Hull Walton, and published by Luxor Press, London, in 1965).

Flagellation has been used in this way for many centuries. A classic treatise on the subject was written by a seventeenth-century physician, John Henry Meibomius. It was called *Tractatus de usu flagrorum in re medica et venerea* (A Treatise on the use of Flogging in Medicine and Venery), first published in 1645 and several times reprinted in later years.

The ancient Egyptians worshipped the god Min or Menu, who presided over fertility and generation; he was depicted as a virile male, naked except for an elaborate head-dress and brandishing a whip. The ancient historian Herodotus tells us that the Egyptians practised flagellation as part of their religious rites; but, as an initiate himself, he was not allowed to mention the reason why these beatings were performed.

There is little doubt, however, about the inner meaning of a phrase which occurs in the letters which passed between those famous romantic lovers of the Middle Ages, Abelard and Heloise: *"Verbera quandoque dabat amor non furor, gratia non ira, quae omnium unguentorum suavitatem transcenderunt"*; "Stripes which, whenever inflicted by love, not by fury but affection, transcended in sweetness every unguent."

During the eighteenth and nineteenth centuries, flagellation was widely, though secretly, indulged in, to such an extent that it became almost fashionable. Indeed, it was whispered that a certain notorious but high-class brothel in London where flagellation was practised, was visited by no less a person than the Prince of Wales, later King George IV. A witty and widely circulated poem, though of doubtful authorship, was devoted to the various pleasures and pains of flagellation. It was called "The Rodiad", and contained a couplet which summed up the social attitudes of many people of high society at that period:

> Delightful sport! Whose never failing charm
> Makes young blood tingle and keeps old blood warm.

Many magical orders and occult brotherhoods have cherished an inner circle where various forms of sexual magic were practised. The initiates of such societies have been sworn to secrecy. However, there can be no rule against quoting something which is already in print, and upon which the copyright has long lapsed.

The late nineteenth century in America saw a remarkable occultist and mystic named Paschal Beverly Randolph. He travelled to Europe and to the Near East, and claimed to be a Rosicrucian. He strove valiantly by his writings to enlighten contemporary society by giving people a higher and happier viewpoint about sexual matters and suffered condemnation by Victorian moralists on that account.

Randolph died in controversial circumstances in 1875. One account of his death says that he committed suicide; but another claims that he was murdered, because his writings had revealed and publicly discussed matters which powerful secret groups wished to remain concealed.

In one of Randolph's major works, *Eulis*, occurs the following plain-spoken passage:

> Remember, O Neophyte, that I am not dealing in mere philosophical formulae; but in, and with, fundamental principles underlying all being. Fix this first principle firmly in your memory: LOVE LIETH AT THE FOUNDATION of all that is. Second, the mystical moment, the instant wherein a portion of man's essential self is planted within the matrix, is the most solemn, serious, powerful and energetic moment he can ever know on earth; and only to be excelled by correspondent instants after he shall have ascended to realms beyond the starry spaces. Third, it follows that as are the people at that moment, so will be that which enters into them from the regions above, beneath, and round about. Wherefore whatsoever male or female shall truly will for, hopefully pray for, and earnestly yearn for, when love pure and holy is in the nuptial ascendant, in form passional, affectional, divine and volitional, that prayer will be granted and boon be given; but the prayer must precede.

Elsewhere in Randolph's works may be found the rationale of this teaching. He likens the human soul to a form of fire, a force which is polarized within the physical body. The negative pole of this soul-force dwells in the brain, while its positive pole is situated in the genital region. Between the two is the life centre, the solar plexus. Through the genital centre, we contact that aspect of the soul which "is in direct magnetic and ethereal contact with the Soul of Being; the foundation-fire of the Universe; with all that vast domain underlying increase, growth, emotion, beauty, power, heat, energy; the sole and base of being, the sub-tending Love, or Fire-floor of Existence. Hence through Love man seizes directly on all that is, and can come into actual contact and *rapport* with every being that feels and loves and dwells within the confines of God's habitable universe." (Quoted from the Manifesto of the Grand Fraternity of the Rose Cross, issued by P. B. Randolph, Supreme Master of the Order, in 1871).

It is possible that there is a connection between the ideas of Randolph and those of the *Ordo Templi Orientis*, the European brotherhood later made famous by Aleister Crowley. In his works, Randolph mentions a mysterious fraternity which he calls "the A.·. A.·. "; and this is the title which Crowley adopted for his supreme occult order. According to Crowley, the initials stand for *Argenteum Astrum*, the Silver Star.

It is almost impossible to talk about the revival of magic in modern times without mentioning Aleister Crowley, the flamboyant, eccentric poet and mystic who gloried in the title of "The Great Beast" and whom the sensational press dubbed "The Wickedest Man in the World". Yet his 'wickedness' mainly consisted of practising sexual magic; which, as we have seen, was nothing new in the western world, either in theory or in practice. On the contrary, ritual sexual intercourse is a very old idea indeed — probably as old as humanity itself.

Obviously, it is the very opposite of promiscuity. Intercourse for ritual purposes should be with a carefully selected partner, at the right time and in the right place. How, indeed, could there be anything truly magical about an act that has been rendered common, tawdry and degraded?

We hear a good deal today about the so-called permissive society. But what in practice does the great permissive society permit? A happy, natural, loving relationship between man and woman — or the flaunting of everything that is ugly, degenerate and eventually repulsive? Its main preoccupation is not so much sex as the commercialisation of sex. And amid all the endless discussion of sexual techniques, what ever happened to love?

It is love and only love that can give sex the spark of magic. Love can take two quite ordinary people, and create something beautiful between them, that no money can buy. To approach *magica sexualis* in a cold-blooded, calculating, clinical manner, is ultimately self-defeating.

One gets the impression from Aleister Crowley's secret magical diaries that he had an approach to sexual magic which was basically of this nature. The old practitioners used to choose a magical partner with great care, and practise only with her, so that a very close bond of affection developed between them. But Crowley would pick up a prostitute and literally use her for some magical rite. Perhaps this is why all his magical enterprises seemed in his lifetime to have little endurance; and his last words were "I am perplexed."

The order in which Crowley learned sexual magic, the *Ordo Templi Orientis*, or Order of the Temple of the East, was founded by a prosperous Viennese business man called Karl Kellner, in 1895. Kellner had previously made a journey to eastern lands, where he had received initiation and instruction from Arab and Hindu teachers. No doubt his status as a Freemason of high grade assisted him to gain entry into circles which might otherwise have remained unknown to him.

Kellner died in mysterious circumstances, in 1905. His place was taken by Theodor Reuss, assisted by Franz Hartmann, the author of a number of books about the Rosicrucians. Another famous occultist, Rudolf Steiner, was at one time a member of the O.T.O. It is evident from the fact that men like this were willing to join the order, that it did not at that time have or deserve the lurid reputation that it eventually acquired.

The O.T.O. kept its inner teachings of sexual magic very secret. In its journal, *The Oriflamme*, a little verse appeared, alluding to this secret teaching:

> Who seeks it, will suffer.
> Who finds it, conceal it.
> Who uses it, let no one know.
> He who is a true philosopher,
> Shall remain unknown.

The order consisted of nine degrees, with a tenth honorary degree bestowed upon the Head of the Order, to denote his office. It was in the eighth and ninth degrees that the secrets of *magica sexualis* were given. However, when Aleister Crowley, on account of his friendship with Theodor Reuss, was made Head of the Order for Britain, he completely rewrote the rituals and added an eleventh degree, which was not in the original scheme of the order.

The teachings of the VIII° instructed in the use of one's own sexual fluids, obtained by ritual masturbation, for the charging of talismans. The IX° taught the magical use of sexual intercourse between man and woman. This was known as the Formula of the Rosy Cross, the cross in this symbolism representing the male genitals and the rose the female.

The basic magical principle behind these rituals is the same as that already described, in the quotations from P.B. Randolph. Its application to the IX° is obvious; and in the auto-erotic VIII°, secret instructions were given under the title *"De nuptiis deorum cum hominibus"*, "Concerning the marriages of the Gods with men". In other words, it was used for the invocation of a particular god or goddess, whom the magician visualized and concentrated on while performing the rite.

Crowley wrote in his Magical Record that he believed these rites worked by somehow moulding circumstances, which were already existing, so that things happened in one way rather than another, as the magician willed. In other words, just as sexual activity can produce a child on the physical plane, so a magical result can be produced upon the subtler planes, which is in a sense the 'child' begotten by the act. This will then manifest upon the physical plane as the circumstance the magician desires.

Sometimes an observation was made of astrological influences and the time for the ritual selected accordingly. A particularly potent time for starting a new magical current, according to magicians of the Golden Dawn tradition, is at the equinox, either of spring or autumn.

We can now get a sufficiently plain idea of the practices which Crowley added in the XI°, because much that could not previously be printed about him has now been published. See *The Great Beast: the Life and Magick of Aleister Crowley*, by John Symonds (MacDonald, London, 1971), and *The Magical Record of the Beast 666*, edited by John Symonds and Kenneth Grant (Duckworth, London, 1972).

These books reveal quite clearly that Crowley had an anal-erotic fixation, as well as a general obsession with nastiness. This is a mental attitude well-known to psychologists and there is nothing 'magical' about it. I only mention it here in order to make it known that the magical uses of sex do not necessarily involve such practices as Crowley indulged in.

Sex is the supreme sacrament, because it is one manifestation of the Great Work, which is the union of opposites. Hence its tremendous potency, for good or ill. We have seen in the ancient Mystery Cults, how the participants in the *Orgia* offered their pleasure to the Gods, believing that it made the Gods happy to see people happy. Some moralists may frown; but surely this was a higher concept of the Godhead than that which pictures God as jealous, vengeful and begrudging of the fulfilment and joy that are the Creator's gift to humanity.

As Charles Godfrey Leland wrote in *Aradia: the Gospel of the Witches* (London, David Nutt, 1899):

> Are not the charms of love of every kind, and the enjoyment of beauty in all its forms in nature, mysteries, miracles, or magical?

VIII
Magic of Dreams

There is one way in which everyone, psychic or otherwise, contacts the unseen world every night. This is the way of dreams.

In all ages this fact has been recognized. The classical Greeks and Romans had legends of two gates to the world of dreams, the gate of ivory and the gate of horn. Through the former, false and illusory dreams came into the minds of sleeping humans; but through the latter, the gate of horn, came those visions which were true, and should be heeded.

The kingdom of sleep is a mysterious realm and full of secrets. Yet it seems so close at hand that we tend to take it for granted. Especially do we accept, in a matter of fact manner, the idea that some dreams have an element of the precognition of future events. This has been proven over and over again by innumerable experiences, both of famous people and of everyday folk. It poses the deepest questions of the nature of time and of the human mind; yet we seldom really think of its implications.

If anyone wishes to prove that the precognitive element in dreams is a fact, this is not difficult. It simply requires concentration and persistence. It is necessary, obviously, to recall one's dreams, so that they can be compared with future events. The best way to do this is to keep a notebook and pencil beside the bed, ready to jot down notes of one's dreams as soon as one awakes.

It will be found that unless recall of this kind is practised, the dream-images will be surprisingly fugitive. It is as if, as soon as normal thinking and reasoning take over, the mind switches itself out of the state in which dreams can be recalled. We have changed gear, so to speak, into another way of using the mind and it cannot successfully function in both ways at once — or not for most people, at any rate.

However, if an effort is made to recall dreams immediately upon waking, but before the mind has completely readjusted itself to the ideas and responsibilities of every day, eventually more and more of our dream-life can be brought into our conscious life for consideration. I am so confident from personal experience that the precognitive faculty will then begin to manifest itself, that I can only say to readers — try it and see.

Sometimes the events thus prefigured are of importance; but much more frequently, they are quite trivial, though of some interest to the recipient. Some experiences of my own may serve to illustrate this.

Some years ago, I was making a particular study of the Qabalah. Books on the subject were not so easily found in those days as they are today, with the present renewal of interest in occult matters. Occult students had to search long and carefully on the shelves of second-hand bookshops, to find anything of real value.

In these circumstances, I had one night a vivid dream. I dreamed that I went to a second-hand bookshop which I often visited in search of books on the occult and there found a book on the Qabalah, which I bought for a moderate price. The book was of unusual size and shape, being large but quite thin, and it was in a red cover.

When I awoke, I remembered the dream clearly, and felt that this was a sign worth following. Accordingly, as soon as possible that day, I hurried to the bookshop. I searched all the likely shelves carefully; but alas, no such book as the one I had seen in my dream was to be found. Ah, well, I thought — just a dream! A pity it did not come true, as this would have been interesting in itself, apart from getting the book.

About a fortnight later, I happened to go into the shop again. There, on the shelf before my eyes, was the book of my dream, answering exactly to its description in size, shape, colour, subject and price. It was in fact Knut Stenring's translation of the Qabalistic treatise called the *Sepher Yetzirah*; and I have it still.

I was not unduly surprised by this phenomenon, as I had

already discovered that I sometimes had precognitive dreams. For instance, during the Second World War I was working in an office in London. One night, I dreamed that I was visiting an old aunt of mine, who lived on the south coast. I found her in a flurry of packing, about to move in haste. I asked her what was the matter, and she replied, in a state of great agitation, 'Get out of London! The Germans are going to start to shell us from the coast on the 13th!'

This was in June 1944, an exciting month, with the D-Day landings imminent. I told the girls at the office what I had dreamed and they laughed. They said I must have been reading the old World War One stories of the Germans' legendary super-gun, Big Bertha, which was supposed to be aimed from France to destroy London. The Germans couldn't possibly shell us from across the Channel.

I had to agree; but I felt uneasy, nevertheless. With the excitement of D-Day, everyone was tensed up. Then shortly after the 13th, we heard that a small German plane had crashed somewhere in London and exploded, doing a lot of damage. We didn't know it at the time; but this was the first flying bomb.

The flying bombs, or V1 and V2 rockets, Hitler's last terrifying weapons of destruction, were launched upon London from across the Channel and one of their main flight-paths was over the place where my aunt, whom I had spoken to in the dream, lived. Official war histories say that the first of them was launched on June 13th, 1944.

The faculty of dreaming true can be an uncomfortable one. One night in recent years, I had a vivid and horrible dream of seeing a man shot down in a sunlit street. I could see and smell the blood; and I was so shocked and upset by it that I mentioned it to a friend of mine who kept a local bookshop, telling her that I was sure there was going to be an assassination. Sure enough, a couple of days later we read in the national press that a United States diplomat had been assassinated in South America. I believe the report said that no less than nine bullets had struck him.

An account of this dream was broadcast over our local radio station, Radio Brighton. The lady who kept the bookshop was good enough to corroborate my statement, that I had told her about the dream before the story appeared in the papers.

I never want to have another dream like that. I felt shaken for days afterwards. Nevertheless, it is interesting from a scientific point of view that the sense of smell entered into it, as well as those of sight and sound, which are usual in dreams. I have also, though not often, experienced taste and touch in dreams.

Usually, I find dreams exciting and enjoyable. I have always dreamed in colour; indeed, I never knew, until I read books about it, that people ever dreamed in anything else. Apparently, according to psychologists, many people only dream in black and white. However, the colours I see in dreams are usually more subtle than those of earth. They often have a quality of softness, a kind of translucence, which is hard to describe; but I have seen something like it in the works of great painters, and wondered if they derived inspiration from their dreams.

There are remarkable stories of people who have been inspired by dreams. Scientists, inventors, musicians, authors and poets — all have paid tribute to the truth of the old saying that "Night unto night showeth knowledge".

Two of the world's most famous weird stories were inspired by dream-experiences of their authors; namely, Robert Louis Stevenson's *Dr Jekyll and Mr Hyde* and Bram Stoker's *Dracula*. Music from the realm of dreams can be heard in Wagner's *Tristan und Isolde*. The composer wrote of this opera in a letter to Mathilde Wesendonk: "For once you are going to hear a dream, a dream that I have made sound . . . I dreamed all this; never could my poor head have invented such a thing purposely." The music of the prelude to Wagner's opera *Das Rheingold* is also based upon material that came to him in a dream.

The story of how Samuel Taylor Coleridge obtained his unfinished poem "Kubla Khan" in a dream is well-known. The poem remains a mere fragment, because while Coleridge was writing it down from memory, he was interrupted by a casual visitor, and he could never afterwards recall it. This illustrates the special nature of dream memories and how they seem to vanish back into the mists of the unconscious unless they are written down immediately upon waking.

We owe the invention of the sewing-machine to a dream that came to Elias Howe (1819-1867). Poor Howe had striven in vain to perfect his idea and was almost destitute, when one night he got a revolutionary new concept in a dream.

The trouble had been where to locate the eye of the sewing-machine needle. Howe had been following the model of the ordinary needle and this had proved unsatisfactory. Then one night he dreamed that he was building a sewing-machine for a savage king in some primitive land. It seemed that the king had given him twenty-four hours to complete the task, on pain of death if he failed. He worked and puzzled, but it was no use. The time was up and he was taken out to be executed. He found himself surrounded by fierce native warriors, all carrying spears. In the blade of each spear was a hole — and immediately he perceived the solution of his problem. The answer was a new kind of needle with its eye in the point. He awoke suddenly and forthwith went to his workshop and started on the design. This is the true story of the invention of the first successful lock-stitch sewing machine.

Closer to our own time is the experience of the atomic physicist, Niels Bohr (1885-1962). Bohr sought to picture the structure of the atom. However, the concept escaped him, until one night he dreamed that he was standing at the centre of a sun. It seemed to be composed of fiercely burning, gaseous matter. All around him revolved the planets of this solar system, which were attached to the central sun by thin filaments. He could hear the planets make a whistling noise as they passed him. Then the bright, gaseous matter seemed to cool and solidify. The planets became motionless, and the idea came to Bohr that what he was seeing was the model of the atom.

From Niels Bohr's dream came the idea of comparing the atom with the electrons revolving about a nucleus, to the solar system. The use of this dream analogy enabled Bohr to win the Nobel Prize in 1922 for his concept of the structure of the atom.

We may note in both these instances that the inspiration did not come without preparation. Both Elias Howe and Niels Bohr had been working hard on their problems before they had the inspirational dream. Their conscious minds had been thinking with great concentration; so that when they slept the unconscious mind took over, solved the problem and presented the answer in the form of symbolism. We too can obtain counsel from our unconscious mind, if we study the symbolism presented by our dreams.

Ever since the days of Artemidorus of Ephesus, in the second century A.D., people have been compiling dream-books, with this idea in mind. The art of interpreting dreams was borrowed by the Greeks from the ancient Egyptians and Chaldeans; and from the Greeks it derives its name of Oneiromancy (from *oneiros*, 'dream', and *manteia*, 'divination'). Artemidorus was the author of one of the oldest and most famous dream-books. Most of the books on dream interpretation in succeeding centuries were based upon his ideas; but such books tended to become more frivolous and superstitious with the passing years, as the occult sciences fell into disrepute.

By the nineteenth century, consulting dream-books had become a popular pastime. Many of these old dream-books still survive; but they are more entertaining than reliable. A better way to learn to interpret dreams is to study dream symbolism for yourself, with reference to the findings of modern psychology. This is, of course, a vast subject; especially when we come to the work of such masters as Carl Gustav Jung. However, the enlightenment we may find if we persevere will take us far beyond the fortune-telling level on which most of the old dream-books were written.

A method of interpreting dreams which is often recommended by psychologists, is that of free association. This means that you think over the symbolism of the dream, and record whatever your mind spontaneously associates with it, however irrelevant such an association may at first appear. This will give you the end of the thread, so to speak, and you can in time acquire sufficient insight to understand something at any rate of what your unconscious mind is trying to tell you.

Suppose, for instance, a young man dreams of walking by the sea. It is getting dark and he watches the moon rise over the water. Then birds start flying round him. They are big, dark-winged, menacing — he gets rather frightened. He looks down, and sees that on his wrist is a golden handcuff. At this point he wakes up. How would one interpret this dream?

For a start, one must always take into consideration the age and sex of the dreamer. The whole point of this dream is that the dreamer is a young, unmarried man. The thing he remembers most clearly is the frightening birds. Birds — birds — what does his mind associate with birds? *Girls*, of course! — it's just a slang term for girls. And the golden handcuff? A pretty obvious symbol of a wedding-ring and the bonds of matrimony, to someone who at the moment doesn't wish to be bound in them. Once one has grasped what the dream is basically about, the rest falls into place. The sea is the unconscious mind itself, the place of instinct and emotion. The moon is a universal mother-symbol.

Yes, mother keeps hinting that he ought to start thinking of getting married. But the dream is telling him that he is not yet emotionally mature enough to take this step; wise advice that both he and his mother would do well to heed.

This brief example may serve as an indication of the way in which modern psychology sets about interpreting people's dreams. It works on a very different principle from that of the old-fashioned dream-books, which merely set out a list of arbitrary meanings which were supposed to apply to everybody, whatever their age or status. Nevertheless, psychologists have found that some symbols do have a general meaning, in whatever dream they occur; hence they have been styled 'universal symbols'.

For instance, the moon very often represents the mother, or feminine influence generally, especially in the dreams of a man; and the sun can represent the father, or masculine influence generally, especially in the dreams of a woman. A road or a railway can mean one's progress through life. The sort of clothes one is wearing in a dream has something to do with one's personality. A hostile entity of some kind, a burglar or bandit, often means one's own repressed tendencies. A stallion, a bull, or other strong, fierce animal, can be one's libido or sexual drive. The sea is the unconscious mind. Water generally is a symbol of emotions. A growing tree means knowledge, especially knowledge of life. The archetypal figure which Jung called "the wise old man" represents the accumulated wisdom of our instinctive inheritance, derived from our ancestors.

Sometimes the dream resolves itself into a sort of play in which the characters are really different aspects of the dreamer's personality; and quite often our unconscious mind makes use of puns and even anagrams to get its message across. To do full justice to this subject would need a book to itself.

To return to the subject of precognition in dreams, that is, the incidence of dreams that foretell the future, this is a matter with which some scientific investigators are now seriously concerning themselves. The new wave of interest started in 1966, when a number of people claimed to have received warnings in dreams about the Aberfan disaster, in which a school was buried beneath a moving mountain of sludge from old mine tips and 116 children were among those who lost their lives. This tragedy which overwhelmed the little Welsh community of Aberfan aroused the pity and horror of the whole country. An article in the *News of the World*, dated 11th December 1966, stated that a senior psychiatrist had collected 72 instances of people claiming to have had premonitions of the disaster, and the Psychophysical Research Unit at Oxford had received 50 such claims. In all, some 200 claims had been examined by this newspaper, from people all over Britain.

Applying the test that the premonition must have been recorded or witnessed to in some way *before* the disaster, the *News of the World* stated that its reporters had been able to authenticate seven definite cases of premonition. Of these, three came in the form of vivid dreams.

Arising from these enquiries, the senior psychiatrist concerned (he was later identified as Dr John Barker) suggested that some sort of early warning system might be set up, with the help of people who had this faculty of receiving premonitions. He thought that a central bureau might be established, to which people could send accounts of premonitions, whether in dreams, visions, or other psychic experiences. If a sufficient number of such accounts were received at any given time, the details of them could be fed into a computer, which would sort them out, see what they had in common and hopefully be able to give some definite warning which could be acted upon.

Dr Barker actually started an organization for this purpose; but unfortunately he did not live to see the full fruition of his work. He died in 1968. However, the idea has been carried on by Mrs Jennifer Preston, who (according to a newspaper report in October 1972) has been running a Premonitions Bureau from her home in Marlborough Lane, Charlton, London. Mrs Preston has collected hundreds of predictions of events, which have been fulfilled too closely for the old explanation of 'coincidence' to be anything but a worn-out phrase.

Two more instances of premonitory dreams may be mentioned which were reported in the national press in recent years.

In May 1968, an East London block of flats, called Ronan Point, partially collapsed after a gas explosion. The collapse was sudden and terrifying, the more so as the flats were new. No one had expected such a thing to happen; no one, that is, except a fifteen-year-old schoolgirl who lived opposite. A short while before the disaster, this young girl had a nightmare, in which she saw the flats falling down, while people screamed and ran for safety. She told her mother about it the next morning and also some school friends and a few people who lived in the block; but at the time no one took the warning seriously. Later, the *Daily Mirror* reported her story, which her mother confirmed.

Suppose people *had* taken the warning seriously? Could such a happening be prevented? If not, what is the reason for such dreams? When we talk about 'seeing the future', what exactly do we mean? Are events already formed in some other dimension, which we may contact while we sleep? Is this process part of what we vaguely call 'fate' or 'destiny' and what the wise men of the East call *Karma*? The faculty of dreaming true raises all these questions and more.

The idea of destiny seems to be especially relevant to another and still more recent case. In April 1973, a heartbreaking disaster hit four Somerset villages, Axbridge, Cheddar, Congresbury and Wrington. The members of the local Ladies' Guild set out in a chartered Vanguard airliner for what was to have been a happy day trip to Switzerland. Their plane encountered severe weather and crashed near

Basle, with the loss of over one hundred lives. Many children were left motherless; and like Aberfan, this was a tragedy which shocked the nation.

One family, however, was spared, because of a dream. According to a report carried by the *Daily Telegraph* on 12th April 1973, a young mother who had booked on the outing changed her mind and returned her ticket to the organizer, saying that she would be satisfied to get only half her money back. She had dreamed that she was in a plane which crashed into trees in a snowstorm and that she saw the bodies of her friends laid out in the snow. These were in fact the circumstances of the crash.

Why was that woman the one to be warned? Did others have such dreams and perhaps disregard them? We do not know the answers to these questions; but I feel that the value of dreams has been put beyond doubt.

IX
Magic of the Weather

All of us, even those who are city-dwellers, are linked to nature by the weather. Our moods respond to sunshine and rain, to a cloudy day or a clear, frosty night. We follow the changing seasons of the year, from Christmas to the first breezes of spring, through high summer to autumn mists, Bonfire Night and winter again. Our ancestors used to do this more consciously, because the succession of seasonal festivals made them able to be partakers in the life of nature. They were part of things, they belonged, instead of being lost and alienated.

Such festivals arose from a deep, instinctive feeling of the oneness of all life. This instinct was the foundation of primitive religion and magic, coupled as it was with the idea that life itself flowed from an unseen divine source, from which all things came and to which all would eventually return.

The idea that mystic and occult links somehow interconnected all things in nature, probably gave rise to the practice of sympathetic magic. What was done as a magical ritual, upon a small scale, would be repeated or reflected in the greater world, if the one who performed the ritual had the knowledge to be able to do it aright and the faith that it would succeed.

A particular instance of this kind of magic may be seen in the ceremonies used by witches to make rain. Reginal Scot describes some of these in his book, *The Discoverie of Witchcraft* (London, 1584); though he treats with scepticism the belief of his contemporaries

> that the elements are obedient to witches, and at their commandment; or that they may at their pleasure send rain, hail, tempests, thunder, lightning; when she being but an old doting woman, casteth a flint stone

over her left shoulder, towards the west, or hurleth a little sea sand up into the element, or wetteth a broom sprig in water, and spinkleth the same in the air; or diggeth a pit in the earth and putting water therein, stirreth it about with her finger; or boileth hogs' bristles; or laieth sticks across upon a bank, where never a drop of water is; or burieth sage till it be rotten; all which things are confessed by witches, and affirmed by writers to be the means that witches use to move extraordinary tempests and rain.

Some of these actions are evidently sympathetic magic, especially the sprinkling of water in the air with a sprig of broom. Broom, or *Planta genista*, is so much associated with witchcraft that it used to be called hagweed, meaning 'witch-weed'. No doubt the sprinkling was accompanied by an invocation to the powers of nature to send rain. The water would have been carried in the witches' cauldron, or taken from a stream which ran from north to south, because such streams were believed to have magical properties.

The flint stone was cast towards the west, in the direction from which, in the British Isles, rain-bearing winds generally come. The idea was to stir up the influences which send rain. The stirring of water in a pit shows the same idea and so does throwing up sea-sand into the air. Such sand would have a natural affinity with water. The other ritual actions are harder to explain, though the boiling of hogs' bristles (no doubt in a cauldron in the open air) may be connected with the old belief that pigs can see the wind. Old country people regarded their pigs as being able to foretell the weather for this reason. If the pigs were unusually lively, running and frisking about, it was a sign that high winds were on the way. A change of the wind usually brings a change of the weather.

The climate of the British Isles is so notoriously changeable that it is often said that we do not have a climate at all — we just have weather. Nevertheless, a great deal of old-time spells and weather-magic seems to be devoted to bringing rain rather than sunshine. Perhaps, in the days before our modern piped water supply, this was the greater necessity.

In the British Museum is preserved a copy of a letter which was sent by the Lord Chamberlain, Philip Herbert, Earl of Pembroke, to the High Sheriff of Staffordshire, in the time of Charles I. It is dated 1st August 1636 and states:

Morris Dancers as shown in an old stained-glass window

> His Majesty taking notice of an opinion entertained in Staffordshire, that the burning of fern doth draw down rain, and being desirous that the country and himself may enjoy fair weather as long as he remains in those parts, His Majesty hath commanded me to write unto you, to cause all burning of fern to be forborne, until His Majesty be passed the country.

The magical performance which is believed to bring fine weather is that of the Morris Dancers. Their tradition is still very much alive in England today and their dancing is also believed to bring good luck generally to the places where it is performed. For instance, at Shoreham in Sussex the local Morris Men dance through the streets early on May Day morning every year. They carry green branches in their hands, and are accompanied by a 'dragon', with snapping jaws, who is a great favourite with the children. The *Shoreham Herald*, reporting on the Shoreham May Day celebrations of 1973, remarked on the large and appreciative audience at the early hour of 6.30 a.m., and noted how once again the event was blessed with fine weather. Perhaps, the reporter suggested, there was something in these old fertility rites after all.

Morris dancing as we know it today dates back at least to the fifteenth century; but it is acknowledged to have its origin in prehistoric ritual. There is nothing airy-fairy about it; on the contrary, it is a very virile performance and needs a high standard of physical fitness and skill in the men who take part. It is essentially a masculine dance, with jingling bells, waving handkerchiefs, the clash of the quarter-staffs (the countryman's traditional weapon) and lively music on the pipe and tabor.

In the North of England, several variations exist, such as the Sword Dancers and the so-called 'Coconut Dancers' — the 'coconuts' being a jocular term for small discs of wood fastened to the dancers' hands, knees and belts. These are rapped together in time to the music, and take the place of the jingling bells worn by Morris Men of the more southern or 'Cotswold' tradition.

The word 'Morris' is of uncertain origin. It is thought to be derived from 'Moorish' and this has led some people to think that the dances were originally brought from Moorish Spain in the days of John of Gaunt. However, it may simply refer to the fact that the dancers often used to blacken their faces in order to preserve their anonymity. Some dancers still do this. It adds an extra touch of mystery to the ritual, rather like the effect of a mask.

We owe a good deal to the late Cecil Sharp for his work in preserving the music and steps of the Morris and other English folk dances. Thanks to him, a revival of interest has taken place this century and in 1934 the Morris Ring of England was formed to keep the good old tradition going.

In his book *Ages Not So Dark* (Privately printed, 1939), the late J. Foster Forbes mentions the Morris Dance, and says: "As to the origin of the term 'MORRIS', I have been assured by that admirable Celtic scholar, Dr Leigh Henry, that it relates to 'the motion of the winds'." Foster Forbes was an unorthodox antiquarian, who sought out all kinds of out-of-the-way knowledge. If this etymology of 'Morris' is correct, it throws quite a new light on why the dance is associated with bringing fine weather.

The power of witches to raise winds is featured in many old tales, especially from Scotland. The late John Gregorson Campbell was a famous collector of these, taking them down first-hand as they were told by old Scottish people. His book *Witchcraft and Second Sight in the Highlands and Islands of Scotland* (Glasgow, 1902), tells several stories of witches who had power over the elements. A famous male witch was 'Macpherson of power' (*Mac-Mhuirich nam buadh*), who came from South Uist. This man was once on a sailing vessel, on a calm day, when the skipper, knowing his reputation, asked him to raise up a wind. Macpherson called for a gentle east wind. The skipper mocked at it and said it was trifling. Macpherson then called for a stronger wind from the north. It began to blow; but the skipper said, "It does not attain to praise yet."

Then Macpherson recited a third incantation:

> If there be a wind in cold hell,
> Devil, send it after us,
> In waves and surges;
> And if one go ashore, let it be I,
> And if two, I and my dog.

Such a great wind blew up that the ship capsized, and all on board were drowned except the wizard and his dog. So says the legend, at any rate; though if it is literally true, it is hard to see who survived to tell the tale, except Macpherson himself.

A widespread belief in the islands of Scotland and the Isle of Man was that witches could sell winds to sailors by means of the charm of a knotted cord. The cord had three knots in it, one for a light breeze, two for a strong wind and three for a gale. The sailor had to undo the knots when out at sea and the wind would blow as required.

Many witches' spells are associated with knotted cords and we still perform a minor spell of this kind when we tie a knot in our handkerchief to remember something. We are tying the thought of what we want to remember into the knot.

There are numerous instances of the belief that somehow human beings and the elements are in a kind of sympathy with each other. Not only do we respond to the weather by being cheered or depressed, but the weather may respond to the deeds of humans. Many dramas of both films and stage have introduced a thunderstorm at some climax of the play. Especially is this so when the action has an occult theme. Storms and magical rites seem somehow to belong together. For instance, old people of the Devonshire countryside used to remark when a storm arose, "Ah, there is a conjuring going on somewhere!"

The great storm which scattered the Spanish Armada was believed to have been raised by magical means. Some have credited the Devonshire witches with having called it up; while others said that Dr John Dee, the occultist who was consulted by Queen Elizabeth I, had a hand in it.

Another furious storm coincided with the death of Oliver Cromwell on 3rd September 1658. It was whispered among Royalist sympathizers that Cromwell had a pact with the Devil and that the Devil had come for his own. They pointed to the fact that his death took place seven years to the day after his decisive victory at the Battle of Worcester. 3rd September also happened to be his birthday and a mysterious coincidence like that was most impressive to those more credulous times.

Perhaps, however, some atmospheric phenomena are more

than coincidence? Both the beginning and the end of the First World War were marked in England by strange weather signs. On the evening of 4th August, 1914, the sun set in a sky so unnaturally deep in its crimson colour as to seem blood-red. I remember my parents describing how the first recruiting meetings were held, against the background of that terrible crimson sky. It seemed like an omen of the trials to come. However, on the morning of the day of peace, 11th November 1918, many people in the Midlands saw an unusual white rainbow spanning the sky. This was commented on in the *Birmingham Mail*, where it was described as "a very rare meteorological phenomenon".

There was an occasion in the Second World War, when a rainbow marked a critical period of the conflict. At dawn on D-Day, just as the Allied troops landed on the beaches of Normandy, a magnificent rainbow arched itself across the battle area. It was much commented on and became known as "the Rainbow of Invasion Morning". An impressive drawing of it by the artist Roland Davies appeared in the issue of *The Sphere* dated 24th June 1944.

Observation of the weather meant a great deal to the country folk of olden days and we may be sure that the village witches specialized in noting weather signs. A close and sympathetic observation of nature, in unspoilt outdoor surroundings, gave them years of experience on which to draw. In this way, they were able to make predictions which to an ordinary person may well have seemed magical.

Many old sayings and proverbs about the weather have been recorded and generations of country folk, though unlettered themselves, must have played a part in transmitting these sayings to posterity. While by no means infallible, it seems likely that they have some grounding in practical observation, to have been preserved for so long. Here is a selection of them:

As the day lengthens,
So the cold strengthens.

The coldest weather comes in after the Winter Solstice, when the days begin to lengthen again.

February, fill the dyke,
Either with the black or white.
If it's the white, it's the better to like.

In this verse, 'black' means rain and 'white', snow. A snowy February brings good weather after it.

March, black ram,
Comes in like a lion, goes out like a lamb.

The 'black ram' is an allusion to the Spring Equinox, when the sun enters the signs of Aries, the Ram.

March winds and April showers
Bring forth May flowers.

Mist in May, and heat in June
Make the harvest come right soon.

Red sky at night, shepherd's delight.
Red sky at morning, shepherd's warning.

The shepherd, who had to spend most of his time out in the open, took the red sunset as a sign of a fine day to follow; but a red sky in the early morning meant rain.

This must surely be one of the oldest weather sayings, because it is noted in the Gospel of St Matthew, Chapter 16, verses 2 and 3:

> He answered and said unto them, When it is evening, ye say, It will be fair weather: for the sky is red.
>
> And in the morning, It will be foul weather today: for the sky is red and lowring. O ye hypocrites, ye can discern the face of the sky; but can ye not discern the signs of the times?

Modern meteorologists have checked on the 'red sky' weather sign and found it to be fairly reliable. It has also been found that the old saying, "A green sky above the sunset foretells rain next day", is based on fact. Certainly within the British Isles, a greenish tinge seen in the sunset sky betokens wet and possibly stormy conditions the next day. So also does a pale yellow sunset.

Another old saw found to be reliable is the one that says:

"When on a dull morning a patch of blue sky appears big enough to make a sailor a pair of trousers, the day will turn out fine." The reason is that this means there is only one layer of low cloud, which is beginning to break up, leaving clear sky above it.

Pale moon doth rain, red moon doth blow,
White moon doth neither rain nor snow.

This refers to the appearance of the full moon. 'Pale' means lacking in light, because obscured by mist.

A ring around the moon,
Rain coming soon.

This phenomenon is known to meteorologists as a corona. It is caused by water droplets in the clouds, which refract the light, and it can also occur around the sun. An even larger and more spectacular ring, seen more often around the sun than around the moon, is called a halo. This is caused by the light shining through high, thin clouds of ice crystals, which have a prismatic effect, displaying a big circle, often of faint rainbow colours.

The solar halo is a beautiful sight, but it is also a very likely harbinger of rain within twenty-four hours. Occasionally, if conditions are right, the solar halo can appear like a cross in the sky, by sending out luminous rays centred on or near the sun. This may be the explanation of a famous phenomenon which appeared on the evening of Good Friday in 1929, when many people in England saw a cross of light shining in the sky. Such, at any rate, may be the *means* by which this sight was made to appear; but that it should be on Good Friday, and no other day, is at least a remarkable coincidence.

If the oak's before the ash,
Then you'll only get a splash.
If the ash precedes the oak,
Then you may expect a soak.

This is an observation about which tree first puts forth its leaves in spring, the oak or the ash, and how much rain we may expect afterwards. Both the oak and the ash were sacred trees in olden times; this may be the reason why they were looked to, as providing an omen for the coming summer.

When the mist comes from the hill,
Then good weather it doth spill.
When the mist comes from the sea,
Then good weather it will be.

'Spill' here means to spoil.

Rain before seven,
Fine before eleven.

A sunshiny shower
Never lasts half an hour.

Mare's tails and mackerel sky,
Not long wet and not long dry.

This refers to a sky full of small, broken clouds.

If on the trees the leaves still hold,
The winter coming will be cold.

Onion's skin very thin,
Mild winter coming in;
Onion's skin thick and tough,
Coming winter cold and rough.

I have met gardeners who firmly believe in this presage; but how does nature adjust itself in this way?

The reason for casting matters of country wisdom in rhyme, was to make them easier to remember. In addition to these scraps of verse, there were other traditions, such as that which called the little herb Scarlet Pimpernell (*Anagallis arvensis*) 'The Poor Man's Weather Glass'. This small, scarlet-flowered weed is a good indicator of likely weather to come, if observed in the morning. If it opens its flowers, it is a good sign; but if the flowers stay closed, it means damp in the air and hence possible rain.

The more active and busy spiders are in building their

webs, the more may fine weather be expected. If rooks are noisy, cawing loudly to each other, it is a sign of rain, and so is the flying of swallows near the ground. Bats flying about on a summer evening are a sign of fine, hot weather the next day.

The deeper the mole digs his hole, the more severe the winter will be. If he digs no more than one foot down, it will be a mild winter; but if he digs deeply, then the further he goes, the worse the weather we shall have.

The more bright red berries, rose hips and hawthorn haws may be seen in the hedges in autumn, the more frost and snow we shall have that winter; because this is nature's provision for the wild birds, against the coming hardship.

Be it dry or be it wet,
The weather will always pay its debt.

In other words, the balance of nature will always somehow be made up; a piece of time-honoured country wisdom that has much philosophy behind it.

It is widely believed that the weather is more likely to change at the four quarters of the moon than at any other time; that is, at new moon, first quarter, full moon and last quarter. Orthodox meteorologists may scoff at any connection between the moon and the weather; but the old idea stubbornly persists.

In the winter, a night sky full of very bright, clear stars is a sign of frost and domestic fires will burn more clearly and brightly in frosty weather. Sensitive people can distinctly smell frost or rain upon the wind; though this is less possible in the polluted air of our cities than it is in the open country.

The great collector of such traditional wisdom and weather lore, rhymes and sayings, as those given above, was Richard Inwards, the grand old man of English meteorology. He lived from 1840 to 1937 and was for many years the most senior and respected member of the Royal Meteorological Society.

In his lifetime he published three editions of his book *Weather Lore: A Collection of Proverbs, Sayings and Rules Concerning the Weather*; the last of which appeared in 1898. He bequeathed the copyright of this treasury of traditional lore to the Royal Meteorological Society and in 1950 a new edition was issued, edited, revised and amplified by E.L. Hawkes, MA, FRAS, the Vice-President of the Society. (Published for the Royal Meteorological Society of London by Rider & Co., London, 1950).

The frontispiece of this new edition shows a photograph of Richard Inwards himself, a bearded, patriarchal figure looking like the reincarnation of an ancient Druid. However, he was no mere eccentric, but one of those extraordinary all-round scholars and inventors that the Victorian era produced so richly. He did everything from exploring the ruins of Tiahuanaco to being a master chessplayer when over eighty years of age. Those of us who love the magic of nature owe him a debt, for his painstaking collection of centuries of countryside tradition, so that we can still profit from it today.

When people become more conscious of natural things, they are bound to take an interest in the weather and respond to its moods. They soon discover, too, that the expression 'the spirit of a place' can be more than a mere figure of speech. Weather to us is a very local phenomenon, in spite of the scientific forecasts now available on radio and television. Without in any way belittling the importance of such forecasts, personal local observation, with the assistance of some at any rate of the old weather maxims given above, will help readers to become weather-wise and provide a constant source of interest and pleasure.

"We shall have weather, whether or not"; and the feel of the rain on one's face, the cry of the wind and the transforming beauty of the snow are as delightful in their own way as the sunshine of high summer. The pattern of a snow crystal under a microscope shows a beautiful six-rayed or six-pointed figure, and out of all the myriads of such crystals, no two are ever precisely alike.

There was an interesting discussion about weather on the *Dimbleby Talk-In* programme on BBC Television in April 1973. The participants were a number of orthodox meteorologists, together with farmers and students of weather folklore. One of the latter remarked that he had noticed for some years past, how four days in the year gave an epitome of what the weather was going to be like for the next quarter. These were Lady Day (25th March), Midsummer Day (24th June),

Michaelmas Day (29th September), and Christmas Day (25th December). As the weather was on those days, so it would generally be for the next three months.

It also appeared from the discussion that there were two dates in the year which gave a reverse forecast. That is, the weather from then on would be the opposite of what it had been like on that day, for a while. These two days are Halloween (31st October), and Candlemas (2nd February).

It will be noticed that the four dates first mentioned are shortly after the equinoxes and solstices; while the other two are ancient Celtic festivals. The reverse forecasts connected with the latter are commemorated in folk-rhymes also. One refers to Halloween and the next day, All Saints or All Hallows, as *Hollantide*, and says:

If ducks do slide at Hollantide,
At Christmas they will swim.
If ducks do swim at Hollantide,
At Christmas they will slide.

In other words, if there is ice on the pond at Hollantide, there will be none at Christmas, and vice versa.

The Candlemas rhyme runs as follows:

If Candlemas Day be fair and bright,
Winter will have another flight;
But if Candlemas Day be clouds and rain,
Winter is gone, and will not come again.

There are several versions of all these old rhymes, which may be found in different parts of England.

During the television discussion mentioned above, a remarkable suggestion was made by Mrs Doris Munday, a hypnotherapist who claims to be able to influence the weather. This lady said that she believed the weather was influenced by people's thoughts. In her opinion, the reason why the BBC's weather forecasts used to be more reliable than they are now, was that when broadcasting first came out, people tended to believe these forecasts implicitly and therefore they came true!

Mrs Munday, who lives in London, was once challenged to

demonstrate her powers by David Frost, who seems appropriately named for taking an interest in weather magic. She responded by causing snow to melt in twelve hours, instead of the usual forty-eight; but the sceptical Mr Frost put it down to coincidence. She also claims to have caused rain at the Olympic Games in Mexico in response to a challenge, to have shifted fog from Luton Airport and to have broken droughts in India and Australia.

Whatever the weather, here is a kindly old saw of good advice to end with:

> After drought cometh rain,
> After pleasure cometh pain;
> But yet it continueth not so.
> For after rain
> Cometh drought again,
> And joy after pain and woe.

X

Magic of the Cards

Many learned volumes have been written about the origin of playing cards; yet this remains one of the world's mysteries. We may feel fairly sure that our present pack derives from the more elaborate Tarot pack. Even so, our simpler four suits of hearts, diamonds, clubs and spades have considerable antiquity of their own.

They seem to have originated in France in about the fifteenth century, when the old Tarot emblems were modified into a simpler pack that was easier to use for gaming. In his book *Playing Cards: The History and Secrets of the Pack* (Spring Books, London), W. Gurney Benham shows how the playing cards we know today have originated from the designs of cards produced at Rouen, France, in about 1567.

The full Tarot pack consists of 78 cards, having in addition to the four suits a suit of trumps, which are a series of symbolic pictures, and having an extra court card, the Knight, in each of the suits. As a result of the revival of interest in occult matters, packs of Tarot cards have again become available at the present day. These cards have long been used on the Continent of Europe for fortune-telling, especially by the gypsies. In England, however, the ordinary playing cards were more frequently used, as Tarot cards were difficult to obtain. Consequently, the playing card pack has acquired an occult lore of its own.

It is a very curious fact that, although the pack of 52 cards was ostensibly produced simply for gaming, it contains a numerical symbolism which is related to the year and to nature.

The four suits correspond to the four seasons: spring, summer, autumn and winter. They also remind us of the four elements and the four winds. The two colours, red and black, represent day and night. The 52 cards represent the 52 weeks of the year. The four suits of thirteen cards each, correspond to the four quarters of the year, each having thirteen weeks. The twelve court cards are analogous to the twelve months of the year; and to the twelve hours between noon and midnight.

The face values, or pips, of each suit, from Ace to ten, add up to 55. If we call the Jack 11, the Queen 12, and the King 13, then the total of pips for each suit is 91. Multiply this by 4, and it gives a grand total for the whole pack of 364 — plus 1, the Joker and we have 365, the number of days in the year!

Furthermore, the four suits of thirteen cards each remind us of the four phases of the moon: new moon, first quarter, full moon and last quarter. These four phases make a lunar month and thirteen lunar months are reckoned to the year.

There are many books today dealing with cartomancy, or divination by cards. Most of them give different sets of meanings for the cards, so that one becomes completely confused. In this book, therefore, I suppose to go back to what, so far as I know, is the oldest set of meanings in print for divination by playing cards, in the English language at any rate.

These meanings and the method of laying out the cards associated with them were given by Robert Chambers in his monumental two-volume work, *The Book of Days: A Miscellany of Popular Antiquities*. The first volume, in which the article "The Folk-Lore of Playing Cards" appears, is dated 1869, and was published by W. & R. Chambers, London and Edinburgh.

Robert Chambers was born in 1802 and according to him he learnt the art of divination by cards from a soldier's wife who took care of him as a child. This would have been about the time of the Napoleonic Wars. If we presume that the soldier's wife had learnt it in her turn when she was younger, then this may be reasonably supposed to take us back at least to the eighteenth century for the origin of this system. Indeed, the meanings given for the cards themselves contain evidence of their antiquity. They refer to dangers from "a duel", or from "death on the scaffold", to which people could only have been exposed in the years before such things were banished by our present system of law. Such card meanings today would

A Card Party in olden days

have to be interpreted in a figurative sense only.

I think it worth while for antiquarian interest to give Robert Chambers' description in his own words. He refers to this method of card-reading as "the English system" and tells us that it is used

> in all British settlements over the globe, and has no doubt been carried thither by soldiers' wives, who, as is well known to the initiated, have ever been considered peculiarly skilful practitioners of the art. Indeed, it is to a soldier's wife that this present exposition of the art is to be attributed. Many years ago the exigencies of a military life, and the ravages of a pestilential epidemic, caused the writer, then a puny but not very young child, to be left for many months in charge of a private soldier's wife, at an out-station in a distant land. The poor woman, though childless herself, proved worthy of the confidence that was placed in her. She was too ignorant to teach her charge to read, yet she taught him the only accomplishment she possessed — the art of "cutting cards", as she termed it; the word cartomancy, in all probability, she had never heard. And though it has not fallen to the writer's lot to practise the art professionally, yet he has not forgotten it, as the following interpretation of the cards will testify.
>
> DIAMONDS
>
> *King*. A man of very fair complexion; quick to anger, but soon appeased.
>
> *Queen*. A very fair woman, fond of gaiety, and a coquette.
>
> *Knave*. A selfish and deceitful relative; fair and false.
>
> *Ten*. Money. Success in honourable business.
>
> *Nine*. A roving disposition, combined with honourable and successful adventure in foreign lands.
>
> *Eight*. A happy prudent marriage, though rather late in life.
>
> *Seven*. Satire. Scandal. Unpleasant business matters.
>
> *Six*. Marriage early in life, succeeded by widowhood.
>
> *Five*. Unexpected news, generally of a good kind.
>
> *Four*. An unfaithful friend. A secret betrayed.
>
> *Trey*. Domestic troubles, quarrels and unhappiness.
>
> *Deuce*. A clandestine engagement. A card of caution.
>
> *Ace*. A wedding ring. An offer of marriage.
>
> HEARTS
>
> *King*. A fair, but not very fair, complexioned man; good natured, but rather obstinate, and, when angered, not easily appeased.
>
> *Queen*. A woman of the same complexion as the king; faithful, prudent, and affectionate.
>
> *Knave*. An unselfish relative. A sincere friend.
>
> *Ten*. Health and happiness, with many children.
>
> *Nine*. Wealth. High position in society. The wish card.
>
> *Eight*. Fine clothes. Pleasure. Mixing in good society. Going to balls, theatres, etc.

Seven. Many good friends.

Six. Honourable courtship.

Five. A present.

Four. Domestic troubles caused by jealousy.

Trey. Poverty, shame and sorrow, caused by imprudence. A card of caution.

Deuce. Success in life, position in society, and a happy marriage, attained by virtuous discretion.

Ace. The house of the person consulting the decrees of fate.

SPADES

King. A man of very dark complexion, ambitious and unscrupulous.

Queen. A very dark complexioned woman, of malicious disposition.A widow.

Knave. A lawyer. A person to be shunned.

Ten. Disgrace; crime; imprisonment. Death on the scaffold. A card of caution.

Nine. Grief; ruin; sickness; death.

Eight. Great danger from imprudence. A card of caution.

Seven. Unexpected poverty caused by the death of a relative. A lean sorrow.

Six. A child. To the unmarried a card of caution.

Five. Great danger from giving way to bad temper. A card of caution.

Four. Sickness.

Trey. A journey by land. Tears.

Deuce. A removal.

Ace. Death; malice; a duel; a general misfortune.

CLUBS

King. A dark complexioned man, though not so dark as the king of spades; upright, true, and affectionate.

Queen. A woman of the same complexion, agreeable, genteel and witty.

Knave. A sincere, but rather hasty-tempered friend.

Ten. Unexpected wealth, through the death of a relative. A fat sorrow.

Nine. Danger caused by drunkenness. A card of caution.

Eight. Danger from covetousness. A card of caution.

Seven. A prison. Danger arising from the opposite sex. A card of caution.

Six. Competence by hard-working industry.

Five. A happy, though not wealthy marriage.

Four. Danger of misfortunes caused by inconstancy, or capricious temper. A card of caution.

Trey. Quarrels. Or in reference to time may signify three years, three months, three weeks, or three days. It also denotes that a person will be married more than once.

Deuce. Vexation, disappointment.

Ace. A letter.

"The foregoing", says Robert Chambers, " is merely the alphabet of the art; the letters, as it were, of the sentences formed by the various combinations of the cards." He then continues with instructions about how the cards are to be laid out and interpreted. The person on whose behalf the cards are being read is represented, if male by the king, and if female by the queen, of the suit which accords with his or her complexion. If a married woman consults the cards, then the king of her own suit represents her husband; and if the consultant is a married man, then the queen of his own suit represents his wife. In the case of single people, however, a lover, whether present or future, is represented by a card of his or her own colouring.

All cards when representing persons, lose what other significations they have. Thus, for instance, the Knave of Spades could represent *either* "a lawyer" *or* "a person to be shunned", *or* the thoughts of the people represented by the King and Queen of Spades. All the knaves represent the thoughts of their respective kings and queens, and consequently the thoughts of the persons whom those kings and queens represent, in accordance with their complexions.

Two exceptions to these rules, however, apply. A man, whatever his complexion, if he wears the uniform of one of the armed forces, should be represented by the King of Diamonds. A widow, whatever her colouring may be, should take as her card the Queen of Spades.

> The Ace of Hearts always denoting the house of the person consulting the decrees of fate, some general rules are applicable to it. Thus the Ace of Clubs signifying a letter, its position, either before or after the Ace of Hearts, shows whether the letter is to be sent to or from the house. The Ace of Diamonds, when close to the Ace of Hearts, foretells a wedding in the house; but the Ace of Spades betokens sickness and death.

The pack of cards should be well shuffled and then cut into three parts by the person for whom the reading is being done. The card-reader then takes up these parts, reassembling the pack, and proceeds to lay out the cards in rows of nine, face upwards. A pack of 52 cards, not being exactly divisible by nine, will thus give five rows of nine cards and one last row of seven cards.

> Nine is the mystical number. Every nine consecutive cards form a separate combination, complete in itself; yet, like a word in a sentence, no more than a fractional part of the grand scroll of fate. Again, every card, something like the octaves in music, is *en rapport* with the ninth card from it; and these ninth cards form other complete combinations of nines, yet parts of the general whole.

So says Robert Chambers, in rather involved and old-fashioned language. In practice, you lay out your pack of cards as described above and then count from the card which is the significator of the person you are reading for. Reckon the card you start from as 'one' and keep counting like this, from one to nine, the ninth card being the first of the next count and so on. Count from left to right, like reading the lines in a book, recommencing at the top if you reach the bottom of the spread. You will find that eventually you come back to the card you started from and this ends that part of the reading.

Note in addition what sort of cards are next to the significant cards and whether they are cards of good omen or ill. They may modify what you have to say about the meaning. Look also at the Knaves, representing people's thoughts, and at the Ace of Hearts, which is the 'house' card. These cards, too, are *en rapport* with the ninth card from them, which may be counted to and read.

The Nine of Hearts is the 'wish-card' and according to whether it is near to your significator or far off, you may deduce whether or not a particular wish is likely to be realized. After the general fortune has been told, another spread may be laid out to enquire if the consultant will obtain some particular wish and the answer is deduced from the position of the Nine of Hearts, as described above.

As with all systems of divination, practice and experience will bring greater facility to the diviner. Frivolous questions will get only frivolous answers. Naturally, a person who has some psychic powers to start with will make the best diviner; but at the same time the practice of divination, if carried out faithfully, will tend to develop psychic gifts.

In describing the practice of cartomancy among the poorer people of his own day, Robert Chambers declared his belief that, on the whole, its practitioners did good. They brought sympathy and consolation to people in distress and often gave good moral advice. Moreover, they did not present their readings as being fatalistic: "They always take care to point out what they term 'the cards of caution', and impressively warn their clients from falling into the dangers those cards foreshadow, but do not positively foretell, for the dangers may be avoided by prudence and circumspection."

This is a wise attitude for the present-day card-reader to adopt also. To delight in filling people's minds with fear, by prophecies of inescapable doom and disaster, is irresponsible. Divination is meant to be helpful; otherwise there is no point in it.

The system of cartomancy given above is certainly a relic of olden days and at the same time eminently practical. Village wise women have used it, and probably the English gypsies also, as the latter seem less acquainted with the Tarot cards than their Continental brothers and sisters.

It may be appropriate, therefore, to end this chapter by describing the correct way to carry out the old custom of 'crossing the gypsy's hand with silver'. This is often referred to, but its real significance is little known. It is really a little ritual to ward off ill-luck, both from the diviner and the person whom the reading is for. Gypsies believe that silver is a sacred and magical metal, which wards off the evil eye. Today, unfortunately, the era of real silver coins is past and the coins we have to use are only an imitation of silver; but that is better than nothing.

The person who is seeking the reading should hold the coin between the thumb and fingers and make with it an X-shaped cross over the gypsy's outstretched palm. Then they should place the coin in the centre of this imagined cross, and leave it not merely as a fee, but as an offering to the spirits who are believed to assist in divination. A true gypsy seer who was approached in this way, even if the enquirer could only afford a silver coin of small value, would try sincerely to give them a psychic message.

XI
Magic of Birds and Animals

An essential part of nature is man's relationship with birds and animals — and indeed with all other things upon this planet. The occult philosophers of ancient time recognized this by ascribing astrological rulerships to the animal kingdom, even as they did to jewels, plants, colours and so on. Likewise, they believed that animals, birds, reptiles and even insects, had curious hidden virtues, which could be utilized in magic.

Unfortunately, this belief often led to acts of callous cruelty by man towards other living creatures, in order to obtain their blood or parts of their bodies for magic spells. Such practices are part of the evil realm of black magic, no matter what excuses the practitioners of them may put forward; and sooner or later the magician who follows this path will find karmic retribution at the end of it.

Let us therefore look, not at such matters as this, but at the fellowship which exists and always has existed, between humans and the rest of the living things we share this planet with. At the present day, we are developing the science of ecology and studying the interdependence of living things and the way in which this interacts with the environment. In times past, however, before such studies existed, mankind had a wordless fellowship, taken for granted, with the animals upon which he depended for food and transport.

Many primitive people have been found to have the idea of a kind of animal-god, who was the invisible ruler and guardian of all the beasts of a certain kind which they hunted. They would therefore not merely slay indiscriminately, but would first ask the guardian of the animals to give them permission to kill some of them for food. After a successful hunt, they would render thanks to the Great Deer, or the Great Buffalo, or whatever the kind of animal involved was, for permitting them to kill the game.

Our ancestors in the Stone Age probably had similar beliefs. We know from their cave-paintings that they practised hunting magic and we find pictures of men upon the walls of the painted caves wearing animal masks and horns and evidently engaged in a kind of ritual dance. Perhaps they are trying to contact the guardian-god of the animals, by thus dressing themselves to look like him. In this way, they are putting themselves *en rapport* with the hidden group-soul of the great beasts, and with its mysterious ruler. They are attuning themselves to the world of nature, in those aspects of it which vitally affect them; for these pictures go back to before the time when man had learned to practise agriculture, to the days when hunting was the mainstay of his life.

The horned head-dress was probably man's earliest form of crown. All the time, archaeologists are discovering more relics of the past which illustrate this. Among the latest to be discovered are the now famous Tassili Frescoes in the Sahara Desert. One of these shows a tall horned god figure, surrounded by animals and humans, with the latter seemingly raising their arms to him in invocation. There is really no need to do as some modern writers have done, and postulate that these ancient drawings represent 'spacemen' with 'antennae' upon their heads. There are too many representations of horned gods and goddesses in ancient art, both primitive and highly cultured, to make such a speculation really tenable.

Right down to the days just before the arrival of Christianity, the Romans honoured Pan, whom they also called Faunus or Silvanus, as the guardian of flocks and herds. He was associated with the goddess Diana, and together they were the rulers of the woodland and of all creatures of the wild.

Pan was a merry, uninhibited old fellow, acknowledged to be from an older stratum of culture than the more dignified gods and goddesses such as Jupiter and his heavenly court. Earthy and orgiastic festivals were held in his honour, notably the famous Lupercalia in the spring, which everyone except long-faced moralists thoroughly enjoyed.

The God Pan, as drawn by Charles Godfrey Leland

Consequently, it was the great god Pan, with his horns and hoofs, his primitive life-force and sexuality, who furnished the model for the Christian image of the Devil or Satan. As the Roman Empire had spread itself over most of Western Europe, the civilization of those countries had been greatly influenced by Roman ways, and the culture of the old gods was everywhere to be found. It did not yield easily to Christianity. People went on clandestinely worshipping the old divinities of nature, who were declared by the new religion to be devils, and their devotees denounced as heretics and witches.

The Greek and Roman Pan found his counterpart among the Celtic people of Europe and the British Isles, as the god Cernunnos, 'the Horned One'. The pagan Romans quite happily accepted that the older, indigenous gods of the native people of their provinces were really just another version of their own gods, as seen through the eyes of a different people. Hence statues and carvings of Cernunnos are found in plenty, showing him as the guardian of animals, the giver of life and fertility and sometimes of wealth. These representations vary from the roughly carved figure in low relief, cut out of sandstone, which comes from Maryport in Cumberland, to the magnificent Gundestrop Cauldron, an elaborately worked vessel of Celtic silver, now in the National Museum at Copenhagen, Denmark.

In later times still, the old Horned One reappears as the god of the witches, worshipped and invoked in the underground witch covens. Sometimes he takes the form of a ram, a bull or a goat; or perhaps these animals are regarded as embodying something of his spirit, as the sacred bulls of Egypt embodied the spirit of Osiris. Sometimes he is impersonated by a man, the high priest of the coven, dressed up in a ceremonial regalia of horned mask and robe of animal skins. Such a figure, seen at midnight in a lonely place, by the flickering blaze of a ritual bonfire, must have been strange and unearthly, even to those who knew there was really a man under the mask.

The psychological effect of masked ceremonies can be very potent, even in broad daylight; as many can testify who have witnessed the strange, old-world atmosphere generated by the famous Obby Oss ceremony held every year in Padstow,

Cornwall, on May Day. The 'Oss' is actually a man in a fantastic mask and a huge black cloak draped over a kind of circular frame. In former days, the man who played the part of the Oss was naked beneath this black canopy, or so it was said. He dances through the little Cornish town, accompanied by traditional songs and general merriment. The streets are decorated with greenery, and many visitors come to see and join in the fun.

Behind it all, however, is a deep meaning. At the climax of the ceremony, the Oss pretends to be killed; only to be resurrected again every year. He is the representative of the old god of the life-force, the power of fertility for humans, animals and all of nature, ever dying and being resurrected from death. He is the ever-renewing cycle of life.

Another piece of folk-magic connected with animals is the Abbots Bromley Horn Dance in Staffordshire. This is still in lively observance each year and has been recently featured in a television film about old English customs. In the course of this broadcast, it was stated that the dancers had to be sure of visiting all the local farms with their performance and music, because it would be unlucky for any farm that was left out. This seems to establish a definite link between the performance of the dance and the bringing of luck and fertility.

Here is a nineteenth-century description of the dance, taken from a book called *Old English Customs Extant at the Present Time: An Account of Local Observance, Festival Customs, and Ancient Ceremonies, yet Surviving in Great Britain*, by P.H. Ditchfield, MA, FSA (George Redway, London, 1896). It has some points of interest not contained in later accounts:

> The annual wakes at Abbot Bromley, a village on the borders of Needwood Forest, near Stafford, is celebrated by a curious survival from mediaeval times called the Horn-dance. Six deer-skulls with antlers, mounted on short poles, are carried about by men grotesquely attired, who caper to a lively tune, and make "the deer", as the antlers are called, dance about. Another quaintly-dressed individual, mounted on a hobby-horse, is at hand with a whip, with which he lashes the deer every now and again in order to keep them moving. Meanwhile a sportsman with a bow and arrow makes believe to shoot the deer. The horn-dance used to take place on certain Sunday mornings at the main entrance to the parish church, when a collection was made for the poor. At the

The Hobby-horse and the "dragon with snapping jaws"

present day the horns are the property of the vicar for the time being, and are kept, with a bow and arrow and the frame of the hobby-horse, in the church tower, together with a curious old pot for collecting money at the dance. It takes place now on the Monday after Wakes Sunday, which is the Sunday next to September 4th. Similar dances formerly took place in other places in the county of Stafford, notably at the county town and Seighford, where they lingered until the beginning of the century. The under-jaw of the hobby-horse is loose, and is worked by a string, so that it "clacks" against the upper-jaw in time with the music. The money is collected by a woman, probably Maid Marion; the archer is doubtless a representation of Robin Hood; and besides these characters there is a jester. Dr Cox has examined the horns, and pronounced them to be reindeer horns.

Dr Plot in his *Natural History of Staffordshire*, published in 1686, gives a similar description of the dance, and he too describes the horns as being those of reindeer. This is strange, because reindeer have long been extinct in Britain; they were last heard of in Caithness, Scotland, in the twelfth century AD.

Some people have explained the Abbots Bromley Horn Dance by saying that it merely relates to the villagers' rights to hunt in the nearby Needwood Forest; but if, as Mr Ditchfield's account states, the dance was at one time performed in other parts of Staffordshire as well, then it evidently has no mere local origin and relates back to something much older and more fundamental than this. It is part of the ancient magic associated with the horned god.

Evidently, too, the present date on which the dance is performed is not that on which it originally took place. Dr Plot describes it as being celebrated "at Christmas (on New Year and Twelfth-day)." This connects the Horn Dance directly with similar commemorations of the horned god which took place in other parts of England at this time; for instance, the 'Christmas Bull', who used to appear in Dorset villages during the twelve days of Christmas, impersonated by a man wearing a horned mask and accompanied by the usual rustic music and merriment. One of these horned masks, called the Dorset Ooser, survived long enough to be photographed and described in *Somerset and Dorset Notes and Queries*, in 1891; and to be noticed by Margaret Murray, in her book *The God of the Witches* (Faber and Faber, London, 1952), as being connected with the worship of the horned god.

The antiquity of this Yuletide masking is proved by the fact that it was denounced in vain by the early Christian church. In England, Theodore, Archbishop of Canterbury, wrote his *Liber Poenitentialis* in the seventh century AD, in which he declared: "If anyone at the Kalends of January goes about as a stag or a bull; that is, making himself into a wild animal and dressing in the skin of a herd animal, and putting on the heads of beasts; those who in such wise transform themselves into the appearance of a wild animal, penance for three years because this is devilish."

The Kalends of January is New Year's Day, the very time that the Abbots Bromley Horn Dance used originally to be performed. It seems that the clergy, being unable to suppress the old ritual, eventually came to terms with it and, according to Dr Plot, used it as an occasion of collecting money to repair the church and give alms to the poor. However, they moved the date of the dance to the annual wakes, or holiday time. Meanwhile, the country people regarded it (and still do) as a survival of primordial magic.

One of the most time-honoured magical practices connected with animals and birds is that of augury. That is, of observing the actions of living creatures, and deciding whether this portends good fortune or ill. The Romans used to take this very seriously, having a College of Augurs, who observed the omens that appeared on any occasion of national importance. The augur wore a white robe, being regarded as a priest of the gods, and he carried a staff called a *lituus*. This was a long wand with a curved piece bending over at the top.

The augur would pray to the gods and then look at the scene through the curved end of his staff. Whatever animal or bird appeared within his view, observed in this way, would be interpreted as the gods' answer to his prayer, according to the meanings laid down by the College of Augurs.

In general, an animal or bird appearing from the right hand side was regarded as fortunate, but one which came from the left was unlucky. This is the derivation of our word 'sinister'. It is the Latin word meaning 'on the left', which foreboded ill.

Many of our beliefs about animals and birds are derived from this old Roman practice of augury. There are still many

Dusio, a mischievous nature spirit, a kind of cheerful hobgoblin

people who do not like to see a single magpie, for instance, because one magpie on its own is unlucky. There is an old rhyme about the magpie which says:

> One for sorrow,
> Two for mirth,
> Three for a wedding,
> Four for a birth,
> Five for silver,
> Six for gold,
> Seven for a secret,
> That's never been told.

Many people, too, are quite afraid of owls, regarding them as uncanny creatures. Personally, I think the owl is a delightful bird and most useful in the way he makes war on rats and mice. Yet the old belief persists that the hooting of an owl, at some unusual time or place, is an evil omen; often it is said to mean news of a death. Probably because it is a bird of the night, with its weird cry and moon-like eyes, the owl is regarded as a bird of witchcraft. Old-fashioned woodcuts, paintings and engravings depicting witches seldom fail to show an owl somewhere in the background. For instance, when Frans Hals painted his portrait of Mallie Babbe, the sorceress of Haarlem, he showed her as a cheerful-looking lady with a tankard in her hand and an owl perched on her shoulder.

However, I doubt whether in real life an owl would often be kept as a witch's familiar. It would hardly make a practical pet and most witches' familiars in this country were (and are) simply pet animals or birds. Their difference from ordinary pets lies in the fact that they are believed to have a special link with their owner and with the spirit world, even to the point of being actually posssessed at times by a spirit.

After all, if the idea is once accepted that human beings can act as mediums for spirits to communicate, why should not an animal be a medium also? Certainly, many people can testify that horses and dogs will react strongly to haunted places and demonstrate their awareness of a spirit presence.

The popular expression about 'rats deserting a sinking ship' is based on an old-time sailors' belief. Back in the days of sail, the sailors swore that if a ship was doomed to be wrecked on her forthcoming voyage, then while she still stood in dock the rats would make their way to the shore across her mooring-ropes, and leave her. Rats and mice were also said to desert a house that was about to be burned down.

There are a number of strange stories on record about unusual behaviour of animals and birds before some natural catastrophe. In October 1923 the people of Tokyo complained of the peculiar restlessness of their dogs. The animals barked and howled with extraordinary noisiness and kept up their disturbed state until early in November. Then they fell silent and all stray dogs seemed to have disappeared — just before the city was struck by a severe earthquake which cost thousands of lives.

A similar thing happened a year before in Copiapo, Chile; only this time the disturbed animals were cats. Hundreds of them deserted the town and fled to the surrounding countryside. Then an earthquake hit the city, doing extensive damage and making thousands of people homeless.

The story goes, too, that before the terrible volcanic explosion on the island of Krakatoa in 1883, animals, birds and even fish deserted the locality. Animals actually leaped into the sea and swam away, to the amazement of onlookers who saw them doing this days beforehand.

In some strange way, animals and birds were believed to have foreknowledge of what was going to happen. Hence, if human beings could communicate with them, they could share this knowledge. One of the legends about King Solomon says that he was given the gift of understanding the languages of animals and birds and this was one way in which he was able to become the great magician that he is portrayed as in Eastern tales.

Such communion, however, does not have to be literally by a language; it can take place by telepathy. If a person is sufficiently sensitive, they can establish a telepathic *rapport* between themselves and an animal.

The famous jungle fighter of World War Two, Lieutenant-Colonel John Williams, earned his nickname of 'Elephant Bill' on account of his extraordinary power to control elephants. When he was fighting in the jungles of Burma, this ability came in very useful. He could also establish a *rapport* with

Three seventeenth-century witches and their familiars.
From an old woodcut

dogs. Often he dared not call a dog aloud, in case the enemy heard him. So he just willed the dog to come to him by telephathy and he said that it never failed up to a distance of two miles.

The more intelligent the animal, the more one can learn from it. Cats are supposed by witches to be particularly knowing and also to have the habit of exchanging information with each other. Hence one reason for the popularity of the cat as a witches' familiar.

Not only did the witch keep a cat herself. She was widely believed to be able to transform herself into the shape of a cat and go about in this disguise whither she would. Other animals, too, featured in this strange belief, notably hares. Many are the folk-tales of the British Isles that tell of the witch-hare. Like the witch-cat, it could be only be shot by a silver bullet; but this was deadly to it and if the fatal shot struck, then not a hare or a cat, but a woman, would be found lying dead. Other versions of the story said that on being struck by a silver bullet, the animal-form would vanish; but later the witch would be found lying dead in her house.

All these stories have a thread of magical correspondence running through them, which may serve to explain them. The cat and the hare are both animals ruled astrologically by the moon and silver is the moon's metal. The moon also rules witchcraft and hence the association. (The importance of the moon in magical matters has already been noted in previous chapters). This also explains the old belief that it is unlucky to have a hare run across your path. The creature might be a witch in disguise.

On board ship, in times past, rabbits and hares might not even be mentioned and some fishermen around Britain's coasts keep to this custom still. Witches were notoriously able to raise storms and talking about witch-animals might somehow arouse uncanny forces and bring bad luck if nothing worse.

It has been known for rival groups of fishermen to take a rather spiteful advantage of this belief, by secretly nailing a rabbit's skin to the mast of their adversaries' boat. Fishermen who found this trick had been done to them would be furious because it meant they dared not put to sea until every scrap of the ill-omened skin had been removed. As the ill-wishers took care to use as many nails as they could, this ceremonial cleansing would take some time; long enough, probably, to make the boat miss the tide while the others sailed off ahead of them.

In spite of their definite psychic sensitivity, one does not often hear of dogs in connection with witchcraft and magic, except for the sinister phantom dog known as Black Shuck. Stories of Black Shuck are found in the folklore of many English counties; but perhaps his favourite haunting ground is East Anglia, an area with strong associations of witchcraft.

He is described as a huge, coal-black hound with fiery eyes, who pads soundlessly by night along lonely lanes, or is seen after dark among the gravestones in ancient churchyards. He is also known as 'Padfoot', from his habit of following benighted travellers.

Further north, in Yorkshire and Derbyshire, he is known as the Barghest, and regarded as a portent of death. In Norfolk, too, he has this reputation and in Cambridgeshire. However, in other places, notably Essex and Lincolnshire, he is regarded as harmless if treated with respect — and the guardian of the good. There are many stories of travellers on lonely roads at night, who have been saved from robbers and ruffians by the apparition of Black Shuck.

Lincolnshire has many traditions of the phantom black dog. There is often some particular place associated with his appearance, such as a clump of trees or the bank of a stream. He generally appears upon the spectator's left and, unlike other ghostly beings, he does not at all mind crossing water. However, he never crosses a parish boundary. He will silently accompany someone along a lane or through a wood, and then vanish when some boundary-mark is reached.

It should be remembered in this connection that old parish boundaries often go back for centuries and that boundary-marks can figure as indicators of what Alfred Watkins described as 'leys' in his book *The Old Straight Track* (first published by Methuen & Co. London in 1925 and several times reprinted). There is not sufficient space available here to go fully into this subject; but present-day researchers who have followed up Alfred Watkins' discovery have come to the

Some of the names given to witches' familiars, according to Matthew Hopkins, Witch-Finder General

conclusion that leys do not merely consist of indications of trackways across the countryside. They also indicate lines of some mysterious kind of energy-flow, which is connected with the fertility of the land. People who travel along a ley are likely to have psychic experiences, especially at a place where two or more leys cross.

This subject, which is well worth investigation, is treated more fully in *The View Over Atlantis*, by John Michell (Garnstone Press, London, 1972). It is also referred to in *Mysterious Britain*, by Janet and Colin Bord (Garnstone Press, London, 1972).

Returning to the subject of the phantom black dog, it is curious to note his resemblances to the Egyptian Anubis, whom the Greeks associated with Hermes. The latter god was the guardian of roads, boundaries and waymarks; and he was also the *psychopompos*, or conductor of the souls of the dead. Anubis, too, was the guardian-god of the dead. He was depicted in Egyptian art as a god with a dog's head, or simply as a large black dog. When Howard Carter opened the tomb of Tutankhamen, there at the entrance to the burial chamber, where he had kept watch and ward throughout the centuries, was a magnificent statue of Anubis in his form as a black dog.

It will be seen how all the things associated with Anubis and Hermes — guardianship, death, way-marks, roads, boundaries — come into the stories about Black Shuck. Perhaps he is an archetypal figure from the collective unconscious of mankind?

Another magical animal which seems to haunt not only the English countryside, but the human mind, is the white horse. It is the favourite subject of Britain's famous and unique hill-figures, formed by removing the upper layers of turf and soil to reveal a different coloured earth, usually white chalk, underneath. For an unknown length of time, the country folk kept these figures in existence, by cleaning and renovating them at regular intervals, generally the magical number of every seven years. This 'scouring', as it was called, was accompanied by a folk festival of rustic games, feasting and dancing.

Nowadays, the white horses and other hill figures are recognized for their interest and antiquity and are generally preserved by archaeological associations. It is now known that

Britain's hill figures were made by the same basic technique as the famous Nazca figures in Peru; that is, by digging trenches and removing the top soil, to show lines of different coloured soil underneath. The so-called 'Candlestick of the Andes' is a similar figure, and not a rock-carving, as it is often described.

Britain's most famous white horse hill figure, and generally thought to be the oldest, is the one at Uffington in Berkshire. Cut on the edge of a beautiful green hill, its white chalk outline resembles the horses depicted in Celtic art, rather than the more naturalistic forms of later hill figures of horses. All kinds of speculations have been advanced to account for this and other British hill figures; but no one really knows their origin and meaning.

The legend of the Uffington White Horse says that it is the white horse of St George, because it was here that he fought and slew the dragon. Below the figure of the horse is an artificial mound called Dragon Hill. It is said that grass will grow very little, if at all, upon the summit of this mound, because of the dragon's poisonous blood which sank into the soil.

Nearby, giving a possible indication of the age of this mysterious figure, is a large enclosure surrounded by a prehistoric earthwork. This enclosure is known as Uffington Castle. Local legend says that if you stand in the centre of the horse's eye, turn round three times, and make a wish, that wish will come true, if sincerely willed from the heart.

St George, the champion of the powers of light against the powers of darkness, is frequently depicted in art as riding upon a white horse. Yet the white horse is rather an ambiguous figure in British folklore. In some places, it is considered unlucky to meet a white horse and the ill luck is averted by spitting on the ground. However, I remember being told as a child that it was lucky to meet a white horse "so long as you didn't see its tail"; in other words, the animal had to be coming towards you, not going away from you. In these circumstances, you could make a wish and hopefully it would come true, so long as you did not look again after the horse had passed you. This may be another relic of the practice of augury, or perhaps a memory of the white horse as a sacred animal in times long past.

Another peculiarity of white horses is that officially they don't exist! However snow-white a horse may be, I am told that horse-breeders will never refer to it as such, but always call it a "light grey". Could this be a relic of some magical taboo?

The magical lore of birds is almost endless and only glimpses of it can be given here. Much of it dates from very ancient times, when our Celtic ancestors held certain birds to be sacred, because they were associated with the gods. The raven, for instance, was the companion of the Celtic god Bran. This may be the reason for the presence of the pet ravens who still live within the precincts of the Tower of London. The magical speaking head of Bran, which continued to discourse although severed from its body, was said to be buried on the site of the Tower of London, with the face towards France, so as to protect Britain from invasion. It remained there until King Arthur had it dug up and removed, saying that he would hold the country by his strength alone. According to Bardic legend, this was one of the three fatal disclosures of Britain.

We know that the Celtic inhabitants of ancient Britain had a custom of carving images of their gods in the form of heads, because many such sacred heads have been found. (See *Pagan Celtic Britain* by Anne Ross: Routledge & Kegan Paul, London, and Columbia University Press, New York, 1967). So this legend may be a folk-memory of the time when a sanctuary of Bran stood upon the site of the Tower of London, until a Christian king did away with it. Yet Bran's sacred ravens are still cared for on the spot, and may be seen calmly surveying the visitors with a superior air, as if they knew all the secrets of the Tower's long and darksome history.

During World War Two the ravens of the Tower were given a special ration of meat, as the raven is a carnivorous bird. Another old legend says that if the ravens ever leave the Tower for good, or their race dies out, it will be fatal to the British royal family.

The cuckoo as the herald of spring was believed also to be able to give omens of people's fate for the coming year. Whatever you were doing when you heard the first cry of the cuckoo would give you an idea of what you would be doing for the rest of the year. The luckiest thing to be doing was to be standing on green grass; but if you heard the cuckoo first while lying in bed, it meant your health was threatened. Hence people used to go out into the country especially to hear the cuckoo, for luck.

The robin and the wren were believed to be sacred birds down to our own day. Anyone who injured them would suffer bad luck for it. There is a charming old saying from Sussex which runs like this:

Robins and wrens
Are God Almighty's friends.
Martins and swallows
Are God Almighty's scholars.

The rhymes may not be very good, but the sentiment is deep and true.

The cock who greets the dawn with his crowing was anciently believed to have the power to disperse evil spirits, who fled at the first cock-crow. Hence the gilded figure of a cock which so often surmounts church steeples and weather vanes. He is there to drive away the evil demons, who were thought of as dwelling invisibly in the air, looking for opportunities to do mischief.

Finally, I like the old rhyme repeated by country people about sowing seeds, which seems to embody the idea that the world of nature is one, and that the birds, like ourselves, are entitled to their share in it:

Four seeds in a hole.
One for the rook, one for the crow,
One to rot and one to grow.
Four seeds in a hole.

XII
Traditional Spells

This collection of traditional spells has been gathered from several different sources. Some of the spells come from old books of magic and folklore; others from manuscript collections. The number of such spells surviving, in print and in manuscript, must be tremendous; but certain broad principles may be discerned, which underlie them all.

Firstly, they are a means of concentrating the mind, by the use of unusual words or actions, upon a certain desired effect. Secondly, they often employ the idea of sympathetic magic — that is, of mimicking the thing one wants to happen, or somehow acting it out symbolically. Thirdly, they make use of the astrological correspondences of things, such as herbs, precious stones, the feathers of birds, or the skins of animals, in the belief that like attracts like.

For instance, things ruled by the Sun, the great light of the heavens, will enable one to become powerful and fortunate; things ruled by Venus, the beautiful evening star and planet of love, will be efficacious in love spells and so on.

There is also the belief that many natural objects have secret magical virtues, and for this reason they are utilized in spells. One can trace this belief from the famous magical treatise called *The Magus*, by Francis Barrett (London, 1801), back to the *Occult Philosophy* of Cornelius Agrippa, the first dated edition of which appeared in 1533, and which had an extensive influence upon magical theory and practice; and back again from Agrippa to the *Natural History* of the Roman writer Pliny, who flourished in the first century AD. Many of the statements made by Barrett were copied from Agrippa, who in turn copied from Pliny.

There exists a very considerable literature of books dealing with this belief in the secret virtues of things and how such virtues could be employed; a belief summed up by old writers under the heading of natural magic. *In herbis, verbis, et lapidibus, magna vis est*, ran the old Latin tag, meaning 'In herbs, words, and stones, there is great power'.

Naturally, only a small selection of these old spells can be given here. They are of antiquarian interest as representing very old beliefs, whether or not they actually worked. Many of them, unfortunately, involved cruel acts towards living creatures; these I have deliberately excluded. I have tried to select those which seemed comparatively harmless, or at any rate not too objectionable to modern standards; so that if any reader cares to try some of them out, not too much damage is likely to result.

Not having tried these old spells personally, however, I must point out that the responsibility is the reader's and that I quote them only as curios of ancient belief.

Here is some advice upon the making of 'suffumigations' or magical incenses, taken from the works of Cornelius Agrippa:

> Fumes made with linseed, flea-bane seed, roots of violets, and parsley, doth make one to foresee things to come, and doth conduce to prophesying.
>
> If of coriander, smallage, henbane and hemlock, be made a fume, spirits will presently come together; hence they are called spirits' herbs.
>
> Also, it is said that a fume made of the root of the reedy herb sagapen, with the juice of hemlock and henbane, and the herb tapsus barbatus, red sanders, and black poppy, makes spirits and strange shapes appear; and if smallage be added to them, the fume chaseth away spirits from any place and destroys their visions.
>
> In like manner, a fume made of calamint, peony, mint, and palma christi, drives away all evil spirits and vain imaginings.
>
> If anyone shall hide gold or silver, or any other precious thing, the Moon being in conjunction with the Sun, and shall fume the hiding-place with coriander, saffron, henbane, smallage and black poppy, of each a like quantity, bruised together, and tempered with the juice of hemlock, that which is so hid shall never be found or taken away; and that spirits shall continually keep it, and if anyone shall endeavour to take it away he shall be hurt by them, and shall fall into a frenzy.
>
> Hermes describes the most powerful fume to be that which is compounded of the seven aromatics, according to the powers of the seven planets — for it receives from Saturn, pepperwort; from Jupiter, nutmeg; from Mars, lignum aloes; from the Sun, mastic; from Venus,

saffron; from Mercury, cinnamon, and from the Moon, myrtle.

If a smooth, shining piece of steel be smeared over with the juice of mugwort, and be made to fume, it will make invoked spirits to be seen in it.'

(A note is necessary here, to point out that some of these herbs, particularly henbane, hemlock, smallage and black poppy, are poisonous and should be handled with care).

Two very famous books of magical secrets are entitled *Les Secrets Admirables du Grand et du Petit Albert* (generally the two volumes are bound together as one). They have been current in French-speaking countries since time immemorial, and are reputed to be the favourite grimoires of witches in the Channel Islands of Jersey, Guernsey, Alderney and Sark.

These treatises are attributed to Albertus Magnus, the famous thirteenth-century churchman and scholar; though he probably had nothing whatever to do with them. One can hardly imagine a sainted bishop (he was officially canonized in 1933) giving what in many cases are magical recipes for very unsaintly purposes. Many different editions of the books exist; from one of them, written in French (no date, but published by Beringos Fratres, Lyon, France), I have translated the following, from the section purporting to give magical secrets in matters of love:

The herb called elecampane (*enula campana*) has great virtues in affairs of love. It has to be gathered while fasting, before sunrise on the eve of St John's Day, in the month of June (in other words, before dawn on midsummer morning, in the night of 23rd-24th June). It must be dried and reduced to powder, with a little ambergris. Then, having carried it for nine days next to your heart, you must endeavour to put a little of it into the food or drink of the person whose love you desire, and the effect will follow.

(The inclusion of ambergris in this love-philtre probably derives from the fact that ambergris was anciently much esteemed as an aphrodisiac. Small quantities, or tinctures of it, used to be put into tea, coffee or chocolate, in the seventeenth and eighteenth centuries, for this reason).

Another spell from Albertus Magnus runs as follows:

How to make the apple of love. You must go one Friday morning, before the rise of the sun, into an apple orchard, and gather from a tree the finest apple that you can find. Then you must write with your own blood, upon a little square of white paper, your name and surname and underneath write the name and surname of the person by whom you wish to be loved; and you must try to obtain three of their hairs, which you must join with three hairs of your own, and use these hairs to bind the little piece of paper on which you have written with your blood. Then you must split the apple in two, and take out the pips; and in their place, you must put the little piece of paper bound with the hairs. Then with two little pointed sticks from a branch of green myrtle, you must carefully rejoin the two halves of the apple (that is, fasten the halves together), and put the apple to dry in an oven, until it becomes hard and without moisture, like the dried apples of Lent. You then wrap it in leaves of bay and myrtle, and you must try to place it underneath the head of the bed where the beloved person sleeps, without them knowing it; and they will soon give you proofs of their love.

If anyone was seriously trying to cast this spell, it would probably be a good idea to tie up the completed 'apple of love' in a little piece of net, so that the whole thing would hold together and the sweet-smelling leaves of bay and myrtle would not become scattered. Also, if writing out both names in full in your own blood seemed too heroic a proceeding, just the initials might be substituted; this would have the added advantage of being less of a give-away if the apple happened by some mischance to be found. A woman casting this spell could, of course, use her menstrual blood, which would probably be very potent for this purpose.

Albertus Magnus believed that there are seven herbs which are especially connected with the seven planets, and are therefore particularly potent in magical work, according to those planets' rulerships. These seven special magical herbs he calls *l'offodilius* for Saturn, *la renouee* for the Sun, *la chrinostate* for the Moon, *l'arnoglosse* for Mars, *la quintefeuille* for Mercury, *l'acharon* for Jupiter, and *le pistorion* for Venus.

From my own researches, I believe the present-day names for these plants to be as follows:

Saturn: Daffodil (*Narcissus pseudonarcissus*).
Sun: Knotgrass (*Polygonum aviculare*).
Moon: Goosefoot (*Chenopodium album*).
Mars: Plaintain (the family *Plantaginaceae*, of which there are several well-known species growing wild in Britain).

Mercury: Cinquefoil (*Potentilla reptans*).
Jupiter: Henbane (*Hyoscyamus niger*).
Venus: Vervain (*Verbena officinalis*).

It will be noted that all of these are common wild flowers, with the exception of henbane and the wild daffodil (the latter being also known by its beautiful old name, the Lent lily). A word of caution is needed with regard to henbane; this is a poisonous plant and should be handled with care. According to Albertus Magnus, it is a lucky herb for men to carry with them who wish to be fortunate in love and enjoy the favours of women. Probably the herb, having been plucked at the correct time as given below, was then made up into a little packet and carried secretly on his person.

Vervain, the herb of Venus, was used in the same way, as a lucky charm. It bestowed enhanced sexual vigour upon those who carried it with them.

The root of the daffodil was recommended as a herb which would put evil spirits to flight. It should be wrapped in clean white linen, and either carried with one or hung up in the house.

To carry knotgrass was a means of contacting the beneficient powers of the Sun and thereby obtaining the good effects of the zodiacal sign in which the Sun was placed in one's horoscope.

Goosefoot, the herb of the Moon, was believed to be a charm to sharpen one's eyesight; because, says Albertus Magnus, our powers of sight are much influenced by the Moon. He may well really have meant clairvoyant sight, because psychic powers are certainly affected by the Moon.

The plantain likewise would be effective in compounding spells relative to the things ruled by the planet Mars; that is, courage, vigour, victory in struggle, enterprise and so on. It is interesting to note in this connection that the plantain herb is known as 'the Englishman's foot', because it is believed to have followed the English wherever they went, throughout the British Empire. This belief is in keeping with the old rulership of the plantain as given by Albertus Magnus.

Cinquefoil, the herb of Mercury, takes its name from the fact that it has five leaflets, and hence somewhat resembles the human hand. Albertus Magnus tells us that if a person carries cinquefoil with them, it will make them clever, and will help them to obtain any favours that they may ask of others.

Albertus Magnus (or whoever really wrote *Les Secrets Admirables du Grand et du Petit Albert*) has some unusual advice about gathering these magical herbs. Most magical practitioners believe that herbs are more potent when gathered at full moon; but Albertus Magnus says that the seven special herbs described above should be gathered from the twenty-third day of the moon until the thirtieth, '*en commencant par Mercure*', which it seems to me must mean that you should gather them during the dark of the moon on the day of Mercury, which is Wednesday. (The days of the moon are counted from new moon, which is the first day. Their number may vary from month to month). As you pluck the herb, you should name its virtues and the use you intend to make of it. Then take the herb, and lay it upon wheat or barley, until the time that you want to use it.

Coming now to traditional countryside spells, we may start with the ancient skills of charming away warts. One old spell tells the sufferer from these troublesome blemishes to go out shortly after the day of the full moon, but while moonlight still lingers, and pick up by moonlight as many small pebbles as they have warts. Touch each wart with a pebble and then tie up the pebbles in a little bundle or bag, made out of a piece of clean rag. Take this out to some lonely place and throw it away over your left shoulder. Come away without looking behind you; and from that day your warts will begin to disappear. The best place to throw away the charmed pebbles is supposed to be a crossroads where three or four ways meet. Anyone who finds such a package should beware, because if they open it, the warts will be transferred to them.

Another version of this spell tells us to take a cinder from the ashes of an open fire and rub each wart with it (a *cold* cinder, of course, is meant, so the charm would probably have been usually done first thing in the morning). Then tie up the cinder in a packet and throw it over your left shoulder at some lonely crossroads, as above, and the warts will leave you. This charm, too, is best worked in the waning moon, which is the time for banishing unwanted things.

One thing is absolutely essential, however, and that is that you must tell no one about it, until the spell has worked and the warts are gone. Nor must you keep looking at the warts to see if the magic is working. On the contrary, you must do your best to dismiss it from your mind, as this gives it the best chance to succeed.

The genuineness of the power to charm warts has been attested to by no less a person than Francis Bacon, Lord Verulam (1561-1626). In his book *Sylva Sylvarum, or a Natural History in Ten Centuries*, he wrote as follows:

> The taking away of warts, by rubbing them with somewhat that afterward is put to waste and consume, is a common experiment; and I do apprehend it the rather, because of mine own experience. I had from my childhood a wart upon one of my fingers; afterwards; when I was about sixteen years old, being then at Paris, there grew upon both my hands a number of warts (at least an hundred), in a month's space; the English Ambassador's lady, who was a woman far from superstition, told me one day she would help me away with my warts; whereupon she got a piece of lard with the skin on, and rubbed the warts all over with the fat side, and amongst the rest, that wart which I had from my childhood; then she nailed the piece of lard with the fat toward the sun, upon a post of her chamber window, which was to the south. The success was, that within five weeks' space all the warts went quite away and that wart which I had so long endured for company; but at the rest I did little marvel, because they came in a short time and might go away in a short time again, but the going of that which had stayed so long doth yet stick with me. They say the like is done by rubbing of warts with a green elder stick, and then burying the stick to rot in muck.

In olden days, nightmares were believed to be caused by evil spirits or black magic. A remedy against such terrors was to hang a large stone with a natural hole through it, on the wall over the head of the sufferer's bed. A large old-fashioned iron or steel key would serve the same purpose. Sometimes both of these things were hung up together. This was also believed to be a way of protecting horses and cattle from bewitchment and uncanny influences. Hence such keys, with a holed stone tied to them, were often to be seen hanging up in stables or cowsheds.

The belief that both people and animals could be adversely affected, either by ill-willing or by the fairies, is reflected in the old Yorkshire rhyme, repeated by country folk half in jest and half in earnest:

From witches and wizards,
And long-tailed buzzards,
And creeping things that run in hedge-bottoms,
Good Lord, deliver us.

This rhyme was supposed to be a protection against all uncanny things, and also against the evil eye. (So too was the practice of carrying a small piece of rowan wood, or mountain ash, in one's purse or pocket. See Chapter III, where the magical virtues of rowan wood have already been mentioned). Presumably the buzzard was regarded as ill-omened because it is a bird of prey.

A popular, but rather more serious and even frightening spell, was one to obtain an apparition of one's future husband, wife or lover. One version of this spell tells the man or woman who wishes thus to obtain a glimpse of the future, to sit alone late on Christmas Eve, between two large mirrors. That is, they must be facing one mirror and have another mirror somewhere behind them. They must have a lighted candle on either side of them and no other lights in the room. Then they must watch until they can see twelve reflected candles, and when this happens, the image of the future lover will appear in the mirror.

It seems evident that auto-hypnosis could play a significant part in this and induce a condition of light trance in which innate clairvoyant power might well produce some manifestation.

Another spell for the same purpose had to be worked when one first saw the new moon after Midsummer's Day (24th June). This was usually worked by girls, though of course a man could do it and vary the words of the spell accordingly. The operator had to go out in the evening twilight to a stile, lean her back upon it and look up at the crescent moon. Then she repeated the words of the charm:

All hail, new moon, all hail to thee!
I prithee, good moon, reveal to me
This night who shall my true love be;
Who he is, and what he wears,
And what he does all months and years.

She would then see a phantom form of her future lover. If nothing appeared, however, the spell had not necessarily failed. She must go to bed without telling anyone of it and she might then see the future lover in a dream.

A third spell of this kind is likewise essentially a piece of moon-magic; because it is worked at the full moon and uses willow, the moon's own tree. Again, this is given as a feminine spell, but a man could use it if he wished. The woman had to go secretly to a willow tree and cut a wand of willow. As always, she must tell no one about it, or the spell would be broken. Then at midnight when the moon was full, she had to slip out of the house without being seen, holding the wand in her left hand. She had to run three times round the house, saying each time, "He that is to be my love, come and catch the other end!" At the third circuit, an apparition of the future lover would appear and seem to take the other end of the outstretched wand.

If it was impossible to run three times round the house, on account of the way it was built, then she must make three circuits as best she could, round the lawn or a nearby field. If she saw nothing, then she should return indoors and hide the willow wand beneath the head of her bed. Something significant would then be communicated to her by a dream.

It is not generally realized that the original purpose of distributing small pieces of wedding cake to friends of the bride and groom after the ceremony, was not only for them to wish good luck to the newly-weds while eating the cake, but also to work a spell. To put a piece of wedding cake under one's pillow, was a way to dream of one's future husband or wife. First, however, you had to borrow a wedding-ring, preferably from someone who was happily married, and pass the little piece of cake through it. Then wrap the cake in clean paper and put it beneath the pillow.

There is a very old belief that onions and garlic will absorb evil influences. For this reason, old-fashioned housewives would never use for food any onions that had been peeled and then left overnight; because they feared that such onions would contain infection or ill luck, which would somehow fall upon the person who ate them.

However, this belief lent itself to spells for banishing evil. If someone had a run of bad luck, and ascribed it to evil spirits or ill-wishing, they could perform the following ritual. Get three small onions, peel them and hang them up separately in convenient places in the house — say, one in the living-room, one in the bedroom and one in the kitchen. The hanging should be done by threading a large needle or bodkin with a piece of red thread and passing it through the onion, then tying the thread to make a loop.

Leave the onions hanging up for seven nights. Then take them down and place each one on a square of clean paper. Sprinkle them well with salt and then wrap them up in the squares of paper and burn them upon a good, bright fire, making sure that they are completely consumed. This will destroy the evil influence.

In the old days, when every house had a large kitchen fire, this was easy. Today, however, many people do not have open fires; but they can still work this spell by throwing the onions into a running stream, or into the sea when the tide is going out. Or they could do the same as is recommended in the wart-charming spells, namely, take the packets to a lonely crossroads, throw them over your left shoulder and come away without looking behind you.

There has always been something magical about the craft of the blacksmith. If you can find a skilled, working smith (and there are still some about today), ask him to take a horseshoe nail and hammer it into a ring for you. You will then have a magical ring more efficacious than any expensive piece of shop-bought jewellery. It will bring you good luck and ward off evil.

The list of traditional charms and spells could be continued almost indefinitely. One principle, however, emerges clearly. That is, that what matters in casting a spell is the amount of personal effort, faith and belief that the person concerned puts into it.

There is a certain old proverb that is true, both for good luck and bad:

There is no one luckier than he who thinks himself so.